PLAYETTE

USA TODAY BESTSELLING AUTHOR
T.L. SMITH

PLAYETTE
T.L Smith

Copyright © 2019

This book is a work of fiction. Any references to real events, real people, and real places are used fictitiously. Other names, characters, places, and incidents are products of the Author's imagination and any resemblance to persons, living or dead, actual events, organizations or places is entirely coincidental.
All rights are reserved. This book is intended for the purchaser of this book ONLY. No part of this book may be reproduced or transmitted in any form or by any means, graphic, electronic, or mechanical, including photocopying, recording, taping, or by any information storage retrieval system, without the express written permission of the Author. All songs, song titles and lyrics contained in this book are the property of the respective songwriters and copyright holders.

Cover design - Wickedly Designed
Editor - Swish Editing
Editor - Edits in Blue.
Proofread - iscream proofreading
Formatted by Integrity Formatting

PLAYETTE

USA TODAY BESTSELLING AUTHOR
T.L. SMITH

Vengeance has a name, and her name is mine.
My role is to take action against the darkest men I've ever come across.
To kill them one at a time.
Until my list is complete.
And in doing so, I'm going to use my most powerful weapon — my body.
They ruined my life, and now it's my turn to destroy theirs.
Even if it means a death sentence for me, each drop of blood will be deserving.
Each kill will be worthy of the price I may need to pay.
My name is Isadora, and my target is the Moretti Mafia.

To all my badass bitches – this one is for you.

CHAPTER 1
Isadora

"ARGHHH."
I cover his mouth with my hand, it's the last thing I want to hear. He bites my hand thinking it's some kind of play but I shake my head at him and say, "Stop it."

He does, exactly as I command. Then he pushes again, biting his lip this time to stop the groaning from leaving his mouth. But then, oh God, it comes out again. "Arghhhh."

It is not even the groan, it's how he does it. He gets this look on his face which makes me wonder why I went back to his house in the first place. The dimple, that perfect hair—I'm sure that's what it was.

As I lay underneath him, he pumps inside me like he's on some kind of mission to build a fence and I am the railings he's hammering into position. It's now I wonder, *Is he really that good looking?* My brain answers quickly, *No, he isn't.*

I needed sex, so I went out on the hunt and this stranger came up to speak to me before I even caught sight of him. He had some cockiness about him that made me think, maybe he would be good in bed.

How wrong I was.

He's up there right now, in the top three worst fucks I've ever had. Losing my virginity was the first, so this is saying something.

I wait for him to finish, because I know he'll come before me. He has that god-awful look on his face and I'm nowhere near done. I'll have to go to the bathroom or wait until I'm home to finish myself off because he sure as shit isn't going to that's for damn sure.

"Arghhh," he groans loudly, his face scrunching up so badly that I have to look away otherwise I'm going to be physically ill, right here, right now.

Turning my head to the side I see a picture of a woman on his nightstand. She's standing next to him looking up at him as if he's everything to her.

Has she slept with him? Because I'm sure if she had she would change her mind.

PLAYETTE

He collapses on top of me. I have to push at him to move and get him off of me. I no longer want his body near me let alone touching mine.

He rolls over and places his hands on his face before he speaks, "You are amazing."

I huff an answer because it's all he deserves while I stand and reach for my dress, and slide it on.

I need to get out of here.

That was terrible.

Turning back to look at him, I find him watching me with intent. "Stay. We can go again."

No fucking way, that dick of his is never coming near me again.

"I have to go." I reach for my purse as a door clicks open in the apartment.

He gets up on his elbows and scrunches his face as he looks to the bedroom door.

"Michael…"

Ah, so that's his name. I never asked. Didn't care. Never do.

"Fuck!" He jumps from the bed naked.

Yeah, he does look good, it's what had me fooled. But looks aren't everything, obviously. Unless your game is vengeance, then you need to look good to carry it out successfully.

"Get in the closet," he says with a look of terror on his face.

I laugh as he opens the door, expecting me to get in. "Not happening," I say turning away from him and opening the bedroom door. When I do, I see the blonde from the photograph standing there, her face has that classic shock written all over it when she sees me. Then when she looks behind me and notices Michael she starts to cry.

"How could you?"

I turn back to look at him. "You cheated?" I ask him.

He nods his head.

Turning back to the girl, I smile. "Do you really want to get fucked by someone who doesn't know how to please a woman for the rest of your life?" I give her a small smile. "I would suggest leaving. Honestly, there's no loss here."

Her mouth opens in shock as I walk past her to the door.

"You bitch," he yells after me. "I fucked you so good."

"Arghhh," I repeat his groan before walking out into the cool night air.

Walking back to my shithole of a place, I wonder if she will stay or will she leave him. Will she accept having the worst sex of her life, forever?

As a little girl I never saw myself where I am right now, never thought this would be my life.

PLAYETTE

Yet, here I am standing out the front of a building I was never even allowed to look at as a kid. Dragging my hand along the metal rail as I make my way up to the strip club where I was hired over a month ago. It's one of *their* places, I haven't seen them around yet. But I am a very patient woman.

Who are *they* you may ask? Well let's just say they're the men who made me who I am today. The woman who only wants one thing, and is doing everything in her power to achieve that end game.

Kill the Moretti Mafia.

"Issy."

Turning my head I notice Heather, who's been at the club not much longer than me, she offers me a wave and a smile. Walking past security and her, I enter the dark club. The place needs a damn good cleaning and possibly disinfection. The private dance rooms need some air fresheners at the very least. Unfortunately, though, I don't think the owners care much.

"Best behavior tonight, Issy. The bosses will be in."

I salute Benny, the DJ as well as manager, of this shithole.

"You got it, boss."

He shakes his head and slides his headphones back on as he adjusts his playlist. The shithole isn't open yet, but it soon will be.

Most of the girls are already here and undressing when I walk out the back to get changed and ready for the night ahead of us.

The girls who go on stage wear extra makeup and less clothing than us. We serve drinks and take orders dressed in a mini skirt with a pink bra. Our bodies are tanned, toned and sparkling to match the club name.

Sparkling — a shit name for a shit club.

But one thing I can't complain about is the pay.

"Issy, you work way too much. Do you ever take a day off? You're making us look bad," Sharon yells out as I slide out of my jeans and pull on my tiny skirt with difficulty because the damn thing fits like a glove.

The club is open seven days a week, all night. I don't want to miss a shift, so in the last month, I've only taken one day off per week. And I make sure the day is one that's going to be slow. A day I hope the owners won't come in. And so far I've been right on the money and they haven't.

Tonight, excitement runs through me as I brush on my bright red lipstick and pull a fake pink wig over my head. Usually, I'd put in some colored contacts, but I don't bother changing my green eyes tonight. However, I work on my tits by pushing them up as high as they will go with my push-up bra and a couple of chicken fillet helpers even though they are huge, then spray

PLAYETTE

glitter over the top.

I paid for a great set of tits when I was eighteen, it was one of the first things I did when I received my inheritance. That was six years ago now, and they have served me well, getting me into the places I need to be for tonight to be possible.

Everything I've worked toward has led me to this point. Close enough where I will be near these men and none of them knowing who I am.

"Girl." One of the girls winks at me as we walk out.

I spot Heather straight away. She wants to go on stage one day but hasn't quite worked up the courage to strip, so she's getting her practice in with serving the men and watching the girls every night.

Some of the girls on stage have confidence others wish for, while the other half drug themselves up so much they don't know their left from their right and that's enough to give them the confidence they need to be there. I don't want to see Heather like that, she's a baby, just turned twenty-one. I realize she's out to conquer this life, while I'm out to destroy it. We couldn't be any more different if we tried, and I think that's why I like her. She's a light to my dark.

"One day soon, Issy. You wait."

I tap her shoulder softly. "Or, you could leave

this place and travel the world," I say back to her.

She raises an eyebrow. "We come from the same background. Do you think girls like us belong out in that world?"

She's right, but she doesn't realize all those lies I feed her about me aren't true. She believes that I come from a trailer town just like her, when that isn't true. I come from a very loving family, one that I cared for more than anything. I trusted and adored them, and that's what makes my vengeance all that much sweeter. Because the people who took that away from me own this club.

And one by one I *will* kill them, each and every last one of the fuckers.

"You can. You can do anything, Heather." I kiss her cheek and walk away. She never had any sort of positive reinforcement growing up. I did and know how it feels. She needs to know that she is enough, and she's more than what this life can provide for her. Heather's goals shouldn't be how she can get rid of stage fright so she can dance for more money, they should be school or travel, something better than this. Anything is better than this shithole.

"Issy, wait up." Heather walks up behind me with a tray in her hand as the club doors open. Guys filter in quickly. This club's never dead, and the mixture of patrons that come through the doors are interesting, to say the least. It's not just

PLAYETTE

old guys, it's also some very attractive younger guys, which makes Heather happy.

"The owners pick two to three girls to go back to their place to serve their guests. I want to be one of them. Be on the good side of them, you know? Can you help me?"

Fuck! I want to scream at her that it's the last place she should be hanging around, but I don't. Instead, I smile and nod my head.

Attachments—I should never make them, but with her I can't seem to help myself.

"Yes, now go before Benny puts you out back." I wink at her. I lied, of course, I will do anything to make sure she isn't picked tonight.

Going to my first table is easy, and the night seems like any other. When time flies by to two a.m. I'm starting to think they won't come in. We close in two hours and tonight isn't as busy as most nights.

"Issy, I need to speak to you." Benny nods his head in the direction of his office, so I follow and shut the door behind me once we've entered. He sits at his desk, his pen in his hand as he writes something on the paper in front of him. "Their cars have pulled up out front, I need you to serve them. Give them whatever it is they want, I don't care what it is. You're one of my best waitresses, you pull as many tips as the girls on stage. So dazzle them with your brilliance, okay? With your best smile."

I give him a simple nod.

He looks at the camera feed showing on the screen next to his desk. "Okay, go."

Spinning around to walk out, as I touch the door handle he calls my name again, so I wait to hear what he says, "Don't fuck this up."

I walk out smiling. I'll show them the best time. And maybe one will even meet his maker tonight.

"You aren't fired, are you?" Heather grabs my hand as she pulls me to the bar. "No." She makes a 'phew' sound and then continues, "It's fine, I can see that's not the case, your smile is too wide. Why are you smiling so big?" I shake my head not wanting to say anything. "Anyway... Oh. My. God," she yells in my ear, I have to cover them from the screech that follows. When I go to say something to her, her eyes are glued on the door. I spin around and watch three men walk in. Each one as dangerous as the next. All covered in tattoos. All killers.

These are the men who murdered my family, and tonight, I'm going to take one of them to the grave as retribution.

"Stay away from them," I say. Pulling my arm free from Heather, I grab the tray as they all take a seat.

"Issy," she calls my name, but I ignore her.

PLAYETTE

Walking over to them, I place on the best fake smile I can muster as I reach them. They all look at me, but only one keeps his eyes on me — he's the one that makes you think about making a dental appointment to ask for teeth as perfect as his.

"What can I get you, gentlemen?"

One snorts, one speaks and it's the one who happens to have a great smile, and the other keeps quiet. "We're anything but gentle, missy."

I've never seen the three of them to this day. My uncle didn't want me to know what they looked like. He believed going in blind's my best option because that way my face can't deceive me. My uncle has known what I want to do since I was old enough to realize it. He was the one who put the idea in my head, and helped me make it a reality.

"That's okay, we don't do gentle in this place anyway. So, what's your poison? Whiskey? Tequila? A beer perhaps?" I ask.

The one who didn't snort and said nothing looks up at me, his eyes are dark brown with a hint of black to them. He assesses me then smiles. His teeth are crooked, but even so, he's still beautiful. All of them are, in their differing ways.

"Whiskey, neat," he finally says.

I offer my best soft smile as I turn away and step to the bar. I reach for my pocket mirror to check my makeup, and when I do I notice he's still watching me, his eyes trained on me. *Just the way I like it.*

"Issy, what do they want?" Benny appears at my side.

"Whiskey."

Benny reaches for the top shelf and hands me a bottle of Macallan with three lowball tumblers.

"Dazzle them," he says, pushing me away.

"What's their names?" I ask as he's glancing over my shoulder.

"The first one, that's Ace. The one with the bald head is Gabe, and the one with the dazzling smile is Carter. He isn't in charge, but he's pretty close to the boss."

I nod, smiling at all that glorious free information. This is the closest I've been to them since I figured out who they are, which I only discovered two months ago. My uncle didn't want me to know too much information too quickly, he said it was best that I find out at the right time and in the right place. The only thing I know about is a tattoo on each of their hands. It has meaning.

The police won't go after them.

They're too powerful.

They own the whole town.

And soon, I plan to bury them in it.

CHAPTER 2
Isadora

"HERE YOU GO, boys." I bend over in front of them, my perfect tits and ass on display. I worked for this ass, I squat every day. This body has been trained and perfected to be a man's dream from the fake boobs to the fake eyelashes, lip fillers, and cheek fillers. You name it I've got it. I am a walking, talking, perfect little plaything.

I just might cut you when you aren't looking.

"What's your name, pretty one?" Brown eyes asks me, he's the one who ordered and his name is Ace. Dazzling smile, who I now know is Carter and is second in charge, watches me. While Gabe, with the bald head, looks around assessing and taking notes on everything.

Gabe's a watcher, I have to remember that.

"Issy." I smile back to him

Ace's hand reaches out and touches my leg. "Why don't you dance for me?"

I didn't expect his touch, nor is it welcomed, but I've talked myself into accepting their touch. Telling myself that it would be just like any of the other guys I've been with. I've been working on ways to try and numb myself to it. But when his hands touch me, something sparks inside me and it takes everything in me to not pull his hand away and scream. *You all killed my family.*

Instead of shaking his hand off I look to Benny who starts walking in our direction. "I've picked the best dancers for you. Issy here… she's just a waitress," Benny says, tapping me on my shoulder as Ace lets go of my leg. His touch is burning my leg, I don't want it there.

"Show me, and I will keep her around," Ace says sitting back, his hand dropping away, the burn that was there all of a sudden gone. Relief washes over my entire body.

Gabe looks to me and then back to the stage.

Sharon steps out dressed in sky-high heels and everything goes black. When the stage lights come on, no one can see anything but her in the middle. She's sitting on a chair, water washing over her white cut-off top like a rainfall, and she starts her dance. All eyes are on her — she's damn good. Better than I could ever have hoped to be.

PLAYETTE

I was trained in dance when I was a little girl. It's the only thing I couldn't bring myself to continue after they passed away. My mother was my biggest cheerleader, and my father never missed a recital.

That's the past, though.

It's no more.

I have to concentrate on the present, and the present is right in front of me.

So close I can taste it.

Walking away, I go to the bar where Heather's watching Sharon work her magic on stage.

"Holy hell, I want to be like her," she says with envy in her beautiful voice. Heather is gorgeously stunning. She doesn't see it though, and that's a problem. I want her to see she can have more—more than this place offers. It's hard when you've been spoken down to your whole life. She told me all about her family and how they used and picked on her, and how the minute she could, she left that trailer and came here. Heather lives in a hotel which charges fuck all to rent a room, and she works as much as I do, so she's saving her money wisely.

"Then do it," I say while reaching for a cigarette.

"You can't have a break yet, you have to serve them." Heather nods to the boys.

With a quick glance over my shoulder I watch

them all transfixed on Sharon's gyrating body and say, "She still has two minutes of dance left. I'll be back in one, ready to serve them." I give her a quick smile.

"Okay." She looks away from me and I slip out the front. I'm not an everyday smoker, more of a 'fuck my nerves are shot' kind of smoker. And right now I need it desperately.

"A lady like you shouldn't be smoking. That shit'll kill you." A voice scares the living daylights out of me making me jump away from the wall. A guy is standing there with a smoke to his lips. I didn't see him, but then again I didn't look. There's never anyone here, only the girls who sneak out here for a cigarette.

"I'm hard to kill," I say lighting it up and taking the first drag.

He doesn't say anything further, but when I turn to look at him, he's already watching me. I can't see him properly as he isn't under the light like I am, which helps him to see every inch of me. "Do you like to stalk strip clubs?" I ask.

He laughs. It's deep and throaty and it matches his voice. "Depends what I need. Today, I need someone, so here I am, out front of a strip club."

I take my time and spend a little longer, but then realize I need to be back inside, so I throw my half-finished cigarette butt to the ground and step on it with my heel. "Good luck getting what

PLAYETTE

you need." I wave him off as I attempt to place my hand on the handle, but his voice stops me before I can pull the door open. Turning to look at him, he steps into the light. Now, if I wasn't a woman on a mission, I would absolutely stay because what I see is one fine specimen of a man. He's not your average looking man. No, not at all. He has a scar just above his lip, his short hair is a medium blond, and he's dressed in a high-end suit. His cheekbones are sharp and strong, and his lips are more than a little kissable.

"What's your name?" he asks.

I smile at him. "My momma taught me to never divulge my name to strangers. Goodbye." I step away because I have a job to do, and this man—no, scratch that—no man, will ever deter me from my goals in this life.

I've come to terms that I may die doing what I need to do.

Vengeance comes in many forms, and in my case, it's worth paying the ultimate sacrifice to achieve. And I'm okay with that. This is why I'm staying away from forming any attachments. Heather might become a problem, but right now, she isn't and hopefully, she stays that way.

Walking past her, I grab the tray which has fresh tumblers with ice and topped with whiskey, and carry them over to the guys who are now talking as Sharon's finished her dance.

"Pretty one, sit, come chat with me." Ace taps his leg reaching for me as I place the tumblers carefully on the table and am pulled directly into his lap. The second time isn't so bad, I'm more prepared now to be touched by these men. I thought I was the first time, but I definitely wasn't, but I have been working on numbing those fears that build up inside me.

"Oh… pretty one, I like the pink hair," Carter says, smiling up at me. "Tell me, pretty one, do you dance?" He points to the stage.

I smile and grab a lock of pink hair to twirl it around my finger in a sexy gesture. "Well, I got moves."

"Show us, pretty one. Get up there and dance for me." Ace slaps my ass as I stand, and I smile, keeping that fake smile glued to my face with the touch of their hands on my body.

As he finishes speaking, Benny walks over with some papers and takes a seat opposite Carter. "Issy, you can go now." He waves me off.

Ace speaks, "No. She's going to dance for us before we leave. Aren't you?"

I look past him to the stage. *Whatever it takes. Whatever it takes.* The floor's still wet from Sharon's performance, but I can work with that.

"Issy isn't a dancer, are you?" Benny states in an attempt to get me out of it.

But honestly, I want to do this.

PLAYETTE

This is my first in.

I need it.

I'm going to take it.

"I am actually."

Benny stares at me as if I just grew a second head.

Maybe I have?

"Since when?"

My smile is big and fake and courageous. "Since... forever. Why don't you play me something slow, Benny?"

The boys clap but it's Ace who speaks next, "Yes, Benny, why don't you go and organize the music."

Benny stands and huffs, his large belly bounces as he walks away. He doesn't argue with these men. When it's just Benny he's the boss, when they're here he's less than nothing.

"Go on, pretty one, show us what you got."

I look around, they're the only customers left. Heather's still standing at the bar with her eyes glued on us. She wants to be me right now, and I'm afraid she may hate me after what I'm about to do. Smiling at her, she offers me a small wave as I step up onto the stage. I don't look at Heather when the music starts as my hips gyrate and my hands roam. The water on the floor forms a puddle due to the lip around the edge which makes it easier to clean, but it proves well for what I have planned. I need to make this better than Sharon, and Sharon's an excellent dancer, one of the best I've ever seen.

Crawling on the floor, my ass moves up and down as I push myself off and my knees slide taking me close to the edge. My skirt is up near my belly and all I'm wearing is a G-string underneath. I undo the buttons slowly, sensually, making it fall away from my body and into the puddle. My hands roam my round, firm breasts and I suck a finger into my mouth before I stand up. The beat of the music becomes stronger and soon my mind takes over my body's movements. I don't look over at them so I have no idea how they're reacting, my body and mind concentrating only on what I'm doing.

It's a magical place.

It's somewhere I've missed.

I'm on the edge of reality and I know I will get lost in it easily.

My pink hair sticks to my face as I come down in a center split and I hear a cheer. Pulling my body forward, I crawl to the edge in an erotic, yet sensual pose. Whistles are becoming louder as the music comes to an end, and when I look up Benny's staring at me with wide eyes.

Reaching for my skirt, I place it back on and climb down from the stage. When I look up, the guy who was outside is standing there in the doorway with a wicked smile, as he watches and

PLAYETTE

my heart skips a beat before he turns and disappears. I blink a few times wondering if I actually saw him there, but then I notice him again by the door.

"What the fuck was that, Issy?" Benny questions while taking my hand.

"Who's that?" I don't answer his question. Instead, I nod toward the guy who's leaving via the front door.

Benny looks, but shakes his head. "Issy, what the fuck was that?"

With a broad smile, I look back at Benny. "I danced."

He throws his hands in the air. "Why didn't you tell me you could dance like that? You just spring shit like that on me?" He shakes his head and I tap on his shoulder to calm him down. Benny seems like an okay kind of guy. He's always respectful to us which we all appreciate.

"You've never asked if I can dance, Benny."

Benny groans as a hand touches me from behind me and lies on my shoulder.

"Pretty one, feel like earning some extra cash tonight?" His hand makes me jump, and I instantly calm down when I know I'm not in danger, yet.

I turn away from Benny, and Ace's hand drops in the process.

Benny has a look of concern written all over

his face which I try to not decipher.

"Yes, of course."

"Good, get dressed. You come with us."

I quickly go out back to change. Keeping my wig on, I change into another small but slightly looser skirt and put on a shirt. This one comes up my belly and barely covers my tits, but ties in the middle. Just as I go to fix my makeup, Heather walks in, and her face shows shock, sadness, and it's not something I think I can deal with right now. I need my head clear for what I'm about to do, and she can't be making me feel bad.

"You… you know how to dance?" I nod putting on a fresh coat of lipstick. "Will you… will you teach me?"

"Heather…" I trail off.

She's looking at me with such hope—who am I to crush that.

"Sure."

Heather claps her hands and wraps her arms around me. "You're my best friend, Issy. I don't know where I'd be without you." I tap her back, not one to cuddle and pull away. "You're going with them, aren't you?"

"It's best you go home, Heather. I'll see you tomorrow." I successfully avoid her question.

CHAPTER 3
Isadora

THEY TAKE ME in their limousine which is all white inside with champagne and crystal glasses neatly stacked on a bench. The guys all talk to themselves on the way over only glancing my way a few times offering me a drink which I decline. Leaving my busted-up crappy car in the parking lot. We continue to head to a high-class neighborhood and a mansion comes into view. Cars are lined up, and they're not your average cars, these are Rolls Royces, Lamborghinis and whatever other high-end cars you can imagine. This place is luxury on steroids.

I glance down at what I'm wearing and cringe.

I'm not dressed for a place like this.

Holding my bag to me for cover and support, Ace steps around the car as a butler, or some shit, opens the door for me. Ace places a hand on my ass to guide me through the double French doors. My nerves are on tenterhooks, I've been preparing for this moment for so long, and to now be in their home and to have access to what I would never have had access to before, my body hums with excitement. Music blares and girls are walking around naked. Men are sitting on seats. There's drinks or drugs in their hand as they watch on, all of them sporting some sort of hard-on tucked away inside their pants.

Ace's hand comes into my view, and when I see the symbol inked in the brighter light, I know exactly what I have to do and what I want to do tonight that will make me feel better.

There are nine members of the Italian Mafia who walked into my parents' little shop that day and killed them. Each one of them had a tattoo between their thumb and index finger—a skull inked in red.

It's a picture I can't seem to erase from my mind.

That's the symbol right there on his hand.

It's the mark I have to look for, it's the mark that I know is responsible for destroying my family.

I eye the other hands and notice all three of them have that exact tattooed symbol. Without

PLAYETTE

realizing it they have made my night a little easier.

"Pretty thing, why don't you change and get ready to dance?" Ace slaps my ass a bit too hard, but I smile anyway dropping my bag to the floor and pulling my shirt off over my head while plastering on a fake smile.

"Tell me where you want me, bad boy."

Ace chuckles and picks me up, throwing me over his shoulder. "This one is mine." He slaps my ass again—*fucker.*

"Ace," a voice booms.

Ace stops in his tracks, places me gently on the floor, and smiles at me. "Stay, I'll be back." I wink and he leans in planting a kiss on my lips. "Fuck, you're beautiful."

I blush at his comment as he turns to leave. He slaps some other girls' asses as he walks past them, and when I look for the other boys they have also disappeared. Pulling my bag up close, I check around. Ace walked out the back, but in front of me is a marble staircase.

To say fear doesn't live in me right now would be a lie.

The what if's are playing games in my head.

What if I get caught?

What if they work out exactly who I am?

What if they work out what I'm doing?

And what I plan to do will warrant my death,

just as they — the mafia — warranted their own death the day they walked into my parents' shop and murdered them.

Shaking my head, I look around, the music's so loud no one hears or pays me any attention as I start up the steps. When I reach the top, I pause at the first door I touch. My heart rate picks up and is now beating out of my chest. If they're behind door number one, I'm not sure what I'll say.

Fuck it! Pushing it open, I find a man fucking two females. He looks back at me and smiles. Quickly, I shut the door.

Walking further down the immaculate hallway, the music starts to slowly fade as I arrive at the second door. When I push on it, I find a man laid back in a chair, a phone in one hand, and his other on his cock. He pumps it up and down rigorously, and I hear the groan of a woman on the other end of the line — he obviously has it on speaker — then his eyes find mine and he stops, and when he does, surprise and something else is written on his face. "Shut the door," he grits out. His cock's still out and hard, while he watches me with intent. I go to step out when his hand wraps back around his cock, and I see the distinctive mark on his hand. I step in shutting the door behind me. "You don't know what you've walked into." The way he says it, it's as if he's warning me. He probably is.

PLAYETTE

But no one has warned him, and I won't give him that courtesy either. "Why don't you grab a drink and come over here and sit on me." He slides his hand up his cock again. Slow rhythmic strokes. The red ink skull shining like a beacon at me. It's teasing me.

Holding onto my bag, I open his small fridge with shaky hands and take for two beers, popping the tops. Keeping my back to him, stealthily I reach inside my bag and pull out a small baggie and drop some of the contents into his bottle. I walk over and hand it to him. He smiles up at me, his teeth are yellow, obviously from smoking, and he's probably the least attractive of the boys I've met so far.

"What's your name, hot stuff?" I ask. I might as well know the name of the man I intend to kill. He takes a sip of the drink with his cock still out. There's no shame in this man, whatsoever, all he cares about is getting off.

"Mack. Now, how about you take them clothes off, and let me see what I'm working with. Or I can do it, with force. It's your choice, girlie."

Well, fuck me, he's one of those. I've met many men like him in my job. Men who like to control the woman, not just sexually but emotionally as well. Pity for him, I won't play his silly games.

"Let's drink first. Then we can play."

The ass throws the contents down his throat, and then chucks the glass bottle behind me. It smashes on the wall and shatters, some of the remaining liquid running down the wall as the glass tinkles onto the carpet. If I stepped back right now, the glass will crunch under the tips of my heels.

"Bitch... strip. Now."

I do as he says, needing to occupy him for just a little longer. He reaches for me when my tits are free and his mouth slides over one of my nipples, he bites and I clench my teeth together to stop myself from screaming. "You like it." It's not a question, it's *his* fact. He pushes a hand up my skirt, slips a finger in and pushes hard. I let him play with me, let his filthy hands which smell of cigarettes and cum roam my body. It's cringe-worthy, but my mind is only registering one result — *the end of him.*

"Why won't you let me play?"

"Bitch, did I ask you to speak?" He pushes his finger in painfully, to the point where I jolt back. He keeps me in place though with his other hand. Clenching my teeth as hard as I can, I play the role he wants me to play.

"I'll please you. Don't you want me to please you?"

He smiles up at me, his mouth making me internally cringe. He pulls his finger out and lays back. His cock still rock hard. "Ride it, bitch."

PLAYETTE

I touch my skirt, looking up at him through my fake pink hair bangs. "Don't you want to watch?" I ask, his eyes sparkle as he sits back on his elbows while eyeing me.

"I'm going to watch you touch yourself, then I'm going to take every hole you have and break you. Do you understand?"

I nod my head, fluttering my lashes at him.

"You'd like that, wouldn't you, bitch?" He strokes his cock again. This guy is fucking dumb, and thinks he's king fucking shit. No wonder he's in the room playing with himself alone, while talking to some online sex worker, while the other boys are having the real thing.

"Oh yes, big boy, I like that." My skirt drops to the floor, and I turn around bending over in my G-string. He has a good view and I can hear his hand working even faster.

"Touch yourself. Now."

I do, my fingers are better than his disgusting ones. And this whole thing just makes me feel dirty now, but I have a mission. Pushing my panties to the side, I slip a finger in and keep bending over watching him from between my legs as I finger fuck myself.

"Harder, bitch."

I speed up my rhythm, while he hastens his hand.

"You're a dirty little slut, aren't you?"

"Oh yes, big boy. So dirty." I look away because otherwise he'll see my eye roll as I smirk. When I look back my fingers pause at the sight of him. Mack's hand has stopped, and his pupils are dilated and his eyes are bulging. I smile, removing my finger and wiping it on his pants, before I pull my skirt down.

"My legs. What the fuck?" He punches his leg a few times while I smile. Then he punches the other one like the dimwit he is. He goes for his phone, but I move fast picking it up and when I look at the screen I see the guy next door with the two girls.

Fuck! He must have some cameras in the rooms or something.

"Are you spying?" I ask while raising an eyebrow.

"What the fuck, bitch. Give me back my phone." His cock's gone flaccid and I smile. "Why are you smiling like that? Go. Get help. You stupid bitch."

I crouch down carefully so as to not touch any of the glass. Reaching for the bottle that touched my lips, I wipe it down thoroughly and place it back on the table. When I turn back to him, it's like he's finally registering what's happening.

"You aren't the smartest cookie in the jar, are you, dear?"

"You." He goes to lift his hands but they flop like a seal's flippers. "What did you give me?"

PLAYETTE

I walk over to him, sitting on the side of his bed, and quickly look around to make sure there isn't a camera in here. That would be bad. Luckily for me, I've picked the pervert's room and he clearly doesn't like an audience on himself.

"You're quite the filthy man, aren't you?"

"Bitch."

I laugh. "I was going to do this quick… cut your throat, maybe."

"They'll kill you."

When I look at him with my green eyes, I grin widely. "I know they will. But first, how many will I get to take with me? You will merely be the first of many."

He spits at me and it lands on my face, the dirty fucker.

"In a few hours, you'll simply go into respiratory failure. If you survive that, I'll let you kill me. But you won't." I stand and turn his music up, placing his phone next to him before reaching for the 'Do Not Disturb' sign and place it on his door as I duck out.

"Goodbye, fuckwit. Die slowly and painfully… it will make me very happy."

He groans and I turn to offer a small wave before I shut the door behind me.

Fixing my wig and checking my clothes, I step down the stairs.

The boys aren't back, yet.

So, I sit and wait, while watching the stairs intently.

CHAPTER 4
Isadora

FINALLY, THEY STEP back in, one hour later. I'm still sitting in the same position, eagerly hoping no one checks on that bastard Mack upstairs. I don't even learn his surname, not that I need to.

Ace steps out, spots me and smiles. "You stayed."

I nod, standing.

"She has to go," Carter states as he walks past me. The music stops as I look past Carter and back to Ace.

"You can find your own ride, right?"

I nod, not sure what to say.

Ace leans in, kisses me on the lips, and pulls back keeping his hand on my face. "Fuck, you're beautiful." His words sound so genuine that I can't help but blush. "I'll be back for you."

I nod, turn and he slaps my ass as I walk out the door with all the other guests who were kicked out as well. I take one last look at the stairs as I step outside, the smile not leaving my mouth at what I've finally achieved, knowing that in a few hours he *will* be dead. And they won't even know.

I call an Uber the minute I hit the street. A few cars stop to give me a lift, but that's not happening. I might have a death wish, but I want to choose how I die and that's not by getting into a stranger's car and being killed. My Uber arrives minutes later, and the drive isn't long before arriving at my temporary apartment. It holds nothing of personal value, just the essentials. I haven't called a place a home since my parents were killed. Nothing ever feels like home, not even my uncle's place. Honestly, he feels more like my Drill Sargent than family.

"You're home late." I jump at his voice.

My uncle's put on so much weight lately, his belly is massive from too much beer, and he doesn't even bother to hide the gray in his hair anymore. I didn't expect him tonight, he lives in a house further away from me. Him sneaking into my space is expected though, he isn't the

PLAYETTE

type to call.

"I met them."

He sits up straighter. "How many?"

"Four. But I killed one of them," I tell him straight up.

He smiles. "Good." His eyes check me over. "You aren't hurt?" he asks with a touch of concern. He doesn't normally show concern for me so I'm confused.

"No, not yet. But it's bound to happen."

He nods in agreement. "You used it?" He nods to my bag.

I pull out the baggie and smile. "Yes. It was quite beautiful the way it worked."

My uncle stands, walks over, and grabs it from me. "Tell me all about it."

A knock on my door startles me, and my Uncle Max slides the baggie back into my hand before he steps over to the back door, turns back to look at me then he slides outside.

Straightening my skirt, I go to the door. "Who is it?"

"It's me, I saw you come in."

I pull the door open to see a smiling Heather. She doesn't wait for an invitation before she pushes in and goes straight for my bed. "I saw you get dropped off. I had to come so you can tell me everything."

"Nothing to tell."

She looks at me, confused. "How is there nothing to tell? You've been gone for a few hours." It's closer to two hours. "Did you sleep with one of them? Perhaps the one that wouldn't stop grabbing you?"

I shake my head. "No, Heather." Reaching for my bag, I place it in my closet so she can't see what's inside.

"I bet you wanted to." She sits forward as if I'm about to tell her every little secret I have. That will never happen.

"No. Now, how about you go back home, Heather. I'm tired and in need of sleep." I omit the fact that I need to wash myself, because I need that guy off of me now. And any reminders of him gone.

"But..."

I shake my head, putting up my hand to quieten her. "Heather... I need to sleep. I'm tired."

She starts to nod her head while standing from my bed.

"Look, maybe tomorrow we can catch up?"

Heather smiles as she walks to the door, opening it. "Issy."

"Yeah."

"Do you think anyone will ever love me?"

Oh shit! My heart cracks a little for her. She comes from such a broken place, I'm afraid I

PLAYETTE

won't be enough to help put her back together. Especially since I'm the more fucked-up of the both of us. I did just kill a man, and I'm not the least bit freaked out about it. If anything I am happy.

"Heather, I love you." Her eyes beam with light. "But I still need you to leave. Sorry, but I have to sleep." She runs to me, throws her arms around my body.

"Thank you, Issy. I love you, too." She pulls back and her smile is so wide that I feel bad. She leaves shortly afterward and I head straight to the bathroom to strip my clothing. Turning the shower on, I step into the scalding water and let it burn my skin, ridding myself of anything that's him.

Having that piece of scum's hands on me made me feel physically sick. The thought of having his fingers inside me seeps into my mind, and it makes me lean over and spew.

I let this happen, it was my choice, but it doesn't make it any easier, though. To have been violated that way, to have his fingers slam inside of me and pretend to him that I was there for him, makes me shudder in so many different ways.

I love sex.

But Mack? Mack is more fucked-up and screwed up than anyone I've ever let touch me.

If I have to deal with something like that again,

I'm not sure I can.

Letting the hot water burn my skin, I sit on the floor until everything else goes numb, replacing one pain with another is all I can think to do. Eyes red, they fill with water, then I let the tears fall, mixing my pain with the shower water.

It's all I can do.

Benny's voice is the first thing I hear when I open my eyes, he's banging on my door so deafeningly and my name's being screeched even louder. Sitting up, I pull my robe around me tightly as I head to open it. When I do, his face is red and his mouth is in a tight thin line. He pushes past me and into the room, while shaking his head he starts pacing back and forth.

"You're going to ruin my already ruined carpet," I say to him.

He looks at me, his eyebrows pinched together then he looks back to the carpet but continues to pace. I take a seat on one of the two seats at a small table waiting for him to speak.

"You…" he pauses while points his finger at me then starts walking again, pacing back and forth.

"Yes. Me…" I say nodding.

He stops again.

"Issy, you've fucked-up real bad."

I sit up straighter.

PLAYETTE

Oh fucking hell! *What does he know?* Shit. What the fuck.

"What are you talking about?"

Benny shakes his head again. "You went with them. Why would you do that?" My back is stiff. "Them… you don't go with them, Issy." He runs his hand through his gray hair. "Fuck, Issy, now they're requesting you and that means I have to find a new waitress. Are you fine with this?"

"They want me back there?" I ask, surprised.

"They do…" He pauses. "This isn't something to be happy about, Issy. You don't know who these men are."

"I have an idea, Benny. You don't need to look after me. I'm pretty capable of doing that all by myself."

"You don't. You have no idea. These men aren't the normal kind that come into the club. They own it. Along with many other things in this town."

"I know."

Benny gives me a pointed look. "You don't. But it is cute that you think you do." He looks around my empty one-bedroom apartment. "You live here? By yourself?" he asks, confused.

"Yes."

"Where are your things?"

"I have things, just not shit. I have my clothes and shoes. It's all I need."

"No photos. No family?" he asks.

"Nope. Just me, Benny." I take a deep breath. "As nice as this is Benny, I need to do things today. Going back to sleep is one of them. Hurry this along, will you?"

"Quit while you are ahead," he says. "You need to leave. I've seen what happens to the girls these boys take interest in, it's never good."

"Thank you for your concern, Benny."

He throws up his hands. "I tried, I really did. But you're just not understanding, Issy. Just know, I've warned you, and you should run." Benny turns, dropping a piece of paper on the table and walking out the door. He turns around, his face is dark, then he slams the door.

Walking over to the note, I notice the address and the time I'm meant to be there. I smile, and sincerely hope I have as much success as I did last night. Every ounce of pain that comes with it, will be worth it. Or so I keep telling myself.

Getting dressed quickly now I'm up, I drive straight to the warehouse my uncle lives in. When I arrive he's up and working on his car. My Uncle Max took me in when I was fourteen, around the time when my parents were killed. He was never a loving man, on the contrary actually. On the day of their funeral, we came back here and he went to work on this car, a car that I think will never be completely renovated. He slides out from under the car when he sees

PLAYETTE

me, then slides back under.

"Run me through it. Step by step."

That isn't going to happen. He doesn't need to know what that man did to me. How his fingers penetrated me in a way I disliked. It had to be done, though. Things have to be done that I don't like to get the revenge I can taste—I want my vengeance and I want it as quickly as I can get it.

Sitting on the bonnet of one of the cars he's been hired to fix, I start at the beginning and skip the dirty details but fill him in on the rest.

"They want me back there tonight," I finish with.

"No. Go to work. Make them chase *you*. A man loves the chase."

"Okay," I reply as he stands.

"You can't slip, Isadora. If you do, it will be catastrophic. I don't want to bury you. It's not something I can do again."

"I know."

My parents death changed him, and not for the better. He was my mother's only living relative. They were close, the best of friends.

"They will try to kill you once they know who you are. You do understand that?" I nod my head. "They won't do it nicely either. They will kill you slowly and painfully."

This fact, I have nightmares about. But my other nightmare became a reality when my parents were killed, it was one I didn't even know I would have at such a young age.

Am I terrified that they will discover me? Yes.

But will that stop me? No.

Because in my eyes it's justified and death will be welcomed when she comes to visit. Even if it involves me being tortured to visit her.

"Do you miss her?" I ask, looking at her photograph hanging on the garage wall, removing all thoughts of my imminent death.

He looks over then his gaze goes down as he shakes his head. "Of course, but you're here. And you are exactly like her."

"Am I?" I ask, a small smile touches my lips.

"You are. And that's why I'm going to ask you to leave right now. I have work to do. There's no time for sentimentality."

CHAPTER 5
Isadora

THE SAME PINK wig I usually wear is firmly on my head, but I still try to straighten it as the music grows louder. Benny smiles when he sees me wearing the usual, short skirt and bra. Heather's not on tonight, thankfully. So, I don't have to worry about her, or what she's doing. She called me earlier to tell me she has plans to stay in, and I told her it was probably for the best.

"You trying to steal my spot?" Sharon pops her hip and places her hand on it.

"What?" I ask, confused.

"That dance you did… you trying to steal my spot?"

"No, of course not."

She eyes me up and down. "If you do, you won't like the outcome." Her hip bumps mine as she walks past me and it almost sends me off balance.

Shaking my head, I go back to work. The night is slow, and halfway through I sneak out for a smoke. When I do I look around for *him,* I notice him leaning against the same wall he was last night.

"Are you stalking, or perhaps you're a serial killer?"

He barks out a slow and deep laugh. I can see him better and what a sight he is.

"Why can't I just be a guy waiting for his girl to finish work?"

"Nope, not buying it." I shake my head.

He steps out more into the light, his hands staying in his pockets as he looks me up and down. "Why do you work here?" He gives a chin lift toward the club.

There's a few restaurants around here, a dodgy hotel across the road where Heather lives, but there's nothing fancy at all. However he's dressed in an Armani suit and looking like he's worth a million bucks.

"It pays the bills," I reply.

He shakes his head and steps closer. "You're lying."

PLAYETTE

I smirk at him, looking up as he inches closer. He lifts a hand to my face, brushes some of my pink hair back behind my ear. "But that's okay, I like liars." He leans down and kisses me ever so softly on my lips. It shocks me so much that I don't even react, I just let a complete stranger kiss me.

He pulls back and starts walking to a black car. The back door opens and before he gets in he looks at me. "Until next time, Issy." He smirks and slides into the car.

My heart rate picks up as I realize I've never told him my name. I made a point of it last night

"Chuckie…" I call out.

The security guard who stands out here turns to face me. "What's up, Is." He gives me a chin lift.

"Do you know who that man is? He's been out here two nights in a row."

"Is, there's been no man. I would've seen him. You come out here once a night for a smoke which you never finish, and it's only you."

I smile at him, tapping his shoulder as I walk back in.

I'm not dreaming him, of that I'm certain.

"Pretty thing." My feet pause as I enter to the loud thumping music. Hands grab and pick me up. Ace chuckles and places me back on the floor. His dark brown eyes stare me down. "Where've you been? You were meant to come to mine."

I check around and see it's just him tonight. This could be a good thing. I place my hand on his shoulder, pressing my lips together, the ones that were just kissed by a complete stranger. One who, for some reason, makes my girl parts sing.

"And how was I meant to get there?" I ask, in the sweetest voice I can muster.

Ace lets me go and scratches his chin looking me over. "That's a good point, pretty. But now I'm here, all your problems are solved."

"Just like that?" I ask playing with him while toying with my pink hair.

"Yes, pretty. I have magical hands which you will soon learn. So, let's go." He picks me up and throws me over his shoulder again. "Benny," he yells out. "I'm taking your best girl with me. Be sure to pay her for a full night."

"She has commitments," Benny replies in a fucked off voice.

"That's all right, Benny. You'll take care of it. Won't you?"

Benny grunts. "Sure."

"See, pretty thing, I got you," he states as he carries me to the door.

I notice Sharon waiting at the bar watching us. "Can you grab my bag?"

Sharon nods and runs off, and when she comes back I'm standing at the door of the car.

PLAYETTE

She looks past me into the car where Ace is sitting. "Can I come?"

I raise an eyebrow at her. "You don't even like me," I say to her. I look down at Ace who's smiling. "Mind if we bring company? She can dance," I say thinking she could be the perfect distraction so I can easily slip out and do what I did last time.

Ace looks up at her. "Yes, my boys love fresh meat."

She doesn't bother going back inside to get her things, she simply climbs into the car squishing me into Ace.

"You guys own the club, right?"

Ace looks over me to Sharon. "In a manner of speaking, yes," he answers. His hand slides on my thigh then pulls up my skirt, his hands are gentle at least.

Sharon watches, her eyes are hungry.

"Do you want him to touch you, Sharon?"

She looks away from my leg to Ace. Sharon's wearing a little dress. Her tits are as fabulous as ever, and are seen through the sheer fabric. Her nipples are hard.

"Yes."

Ace grabs my face and turns my head to face him. He kisses my lips, hard. I get over the shock fast as his lips start moving. He isn't a bad kisser, but he isn't a great kisser either. His lips are smashed against mine, and there's no tenderness in his kiss at all. I've been kissed by a lot of frogs, I've slept with a lot of men. And I knew my sex appeal would be what would get me into the place with these men, and I was right.

Sex and me, we're old friends.

And I love it.

The power you can hold over a man. The control you can gain if you use it correctly. You can make a man, a powerful man, blind to everything around him if you choose to and do it right.

And I choose to.

Opening my eyes, I see Ace's are already open and staring at Sharon as he kisses me. I pull away, lean over her and bend so my ass is in his face. Sharon slides over to my position as Ace's hand grabs my ass.

"Fuck."

She doesn't waste any time kissing him as the car comes to a stop. I'm the first to exit taking my bag with me as I slide out. Walking around to their side, I wait until they get out.

Sharon has a look of pure excitement written all over her face. How? Well, I don't even understand. Even if I wasn't trying to get into this place to kill every last one of them, I would never choose to come here.

A gunshot rings out and Sharon jumps. My

PLAYETTE

eyes go to where the sound came from and Ace chuckles.

"I'll keep you safe. The only big bad you need to watch out for is me."

I giggle as I slide my arm through his. We walk inside and he guides us to the staircase that leads up. When we pass the first door my palms begin to get sweaty, and when we reach the second door he stops, reading the 'Do Not Disturb' sign.

"Ace, you aren't stealing our company for the night, now, are you?"

Turning around to a perfect smile being pushed our way, I see Carter leaning against the wall. Ace flicks the door open anyway and nods for us to enter. It's damn dark. So, Sharon reaches for the light and flicks it on, and then she screams so loudly my ears ring as I stand there trying to hide my smile.

"What on earth, woman," Carter says looking to Ace. "You bring a broken one?"

Walking into the room, pushing Ace and I backward, Carter says one simple word, "Fuck."

Ace steps in, and I follow closely behind so I can see. There the fucker is, lying on the bed, eyes wide open, not breathing. No one knew he was there for a good twenty-four hours. Enough time for the drug to kick in and kill him. He had no chance. Carter runs over, his hand goes to his chest, but we all know before he even starts CPR that he's dead.

No one who's alive looks like that—gray pasty skin, mouth hanging open, death stare, and a smell that is acrid to my senses.

"Ben. Come on, man," Carter says pushing again.

"Who's that?" I ask Ace, and I'm more than a little surprised when he answers.

"That's his brother," Ace replies.

Carter tries furiously pushing on Mack's chest. I can see it now, the resemblance. Granted Carter's way better looking, but as he tries to revive his extremely dead brother, I don't feel a touch of guilt or an ounce of sympathy and definitely no remorse. I've done the world a favor by taking him off this planet.

"You girls best wait downstairs, the boss won't be happy about this."

I reach for a frozen Sharon and pull on her arm, so she turns, but she falls and trips, her hands landing on the broken glass from the night before when Mack threw the bottle. Blood begins to seep from the cuts in her hands and Ace swears. He looks at me, all lust gone now from his dark brown eyes. "Clean her the fuck up…" he pauses, "… downstairs."

I pull her up and out and he shuts the door. Sharon looks at her bleeding hands shaking her head, but she really doesn't seem to be all there

PLAYETTE

at the moment. "This is bad." It's all she says as tears start leaving her eyes and run down her cheeks. I wipe them away feeling somewhat responsible for this mess she's found herself in.

"I'll bandage them up. It'll be fine."

She shakes her head. "No, it won't. I need them to dance. How am I meant to dance the pole with injured hands?"

I look at them, and notice they're bleeding heavily now and probably need stitching. We reach the bottom step, and I pull her into the kitchen. Wrapping a cloth I find folded on the bench around her hand, I position her on the counter. "Wait here, while I try to find something else." Before I can walk away, another girl steps in holding a first aid kit, and hands it to me. She's young, actually younger than Heather.

"Thanks," I mutter.

She looks to Sharon's hands and shakes her head. "What happened up there?" she asks, her head nodding to the stairs we just came down from.

"Some guy's dead up there, on the bed," Sharon says.

"Mack?" she asks.

I nod my head.

She smiles.

There's no sadness in her eyes at all, if anything I think she's happy about it.

"Good. He was mean. So mean." She looks at her wrists, and I see bruises there.

"What did he do to you?" I ask.

She glances back over her shoulder. "He did it to all the girls. The animal likes forceful sex." She shivers as the words leave her mouth.

"I'm sorry."

She looks down and I look away trying not to catch her eyes again so she will be able to compose herself. Opening the kit, I start fixing Sharon's hands.

"Who's the boss?" Sharon asks.

The little thing perks up at that. "That's Jasper. He doesn't play all the time like the boys do, though. He's more…" she pauses lost in thought, "… serious."

"Are they mafia?" Sharon tries to whisper, but it's barely a whisper considering we all hear her.

"They are."

I smile already knowing this—the Italian Mafia to be exact. Some may look sweet, but they will kill you if you cross them, sometimes for even just looking at them. They're anything but damn sweet.

"Are we safe to be here?" Sharon whispers again while looking around.

"Tell me more about Jasper? Where is he?" I ask, ignoring Sharon's words.

The young girl looks me up and down. "You

PLAYETTE

should go and not look back." She walks away leaving us, and Sharon grabs my hand. "I want to leave, please," she begs.

I nod, walking her out.

CHAPTER 6
Isadora

"We shouldn't have gone there," Sharon says, looking at her hands and then back to me.

"No. *You* shouldn't have…" I pause. "Now, I have to go home," I say.

"You're not making any sense. What are you up to?"

I turn to look at her, her long blonde hair doesn't match my brown hair, which is covered by my pink wig. I decide not to answer her. I shouldn't have brought her, I don't even like her. Guess she was there to play a part, that part being so I could gain access to the men while she was a distraction. It didn't work tonight.

As we arrive at the club, I usher her out. She walks inside while I pay the driver who leaves me where I stand. I could go inside and keep working, I guess, but now I'll have to figure out how I'm getting back to that place to mark my next kill.

"So pretty in pink." His voice startles me.

I jump on the spot. "No smoke tonight?"

He bites his lip as he looks me over, the scar stretches and he smirks at me. His chocolate hair is styled to perfection and tonight he's wearing jeans with a black shirt. He looks good, real good. My eyes search around and I see his black car sitting not far from the club's entrance.

"Why do you come here?" I ask, stepping closer. He does as well. His smirk not leaving his face, while his hands don't leave his pockets either.

"So, can I kiss you?"

My heart rate picks up. I nod back to the club. "You could go in there with the right amount of cash, and have any of them kiss you."

"Including you?" he dares ask me.

"No. I don't kiss for money."

"But, would you do other things?" he asks, his head dropping to the side with the innuendo.

"No," I answer truthfully.

I'm in this business for one reason and one reason only — to get to them.

PLAYETTE

"Such a shame, really. Such a shame." He shakes his head and starts walking backward to his car. "Would you like to come with me?" He opens the door.

I look at it and shake my head. "No woman should get in a car with a stranger," I reply, but with a smile.

He taps his chin with his finger. "Then, why did you?"

"Excuse me?" I ask.

"You got in the car with them, I saw you. So, why did you?"

"How do you know I don't know *them?*"

"Do you?" he challenges.

"No," I answer truthfully.

"Well, why won't you get in mine?"

"Agendas," I say, smiling.

"So, you have an agenda to get into theirs, but you don't mine?" That smirk is back again.

"What do you want from me?"

His eyes travel the length of me. "What can you give?"

I smile back at him. "Nothing. Now, goodnight, stalking stranger."

"At least leave me with a parting kiss?" he says loud enough for me to stop in my tracks. "I can still taste you, Issy. Can you taste me?"

I spin around to face him. "How do you know

my name?"

He smirks. "Does that matter?"

I nod my head. "Of course it does."

"Kiss me, and I will tell you."

"A kiss?" I ask, confused. "And you will tell me how you know my name?" I question with a laugh. "No, thanks." I turn to walk away again.

"If that is your will, then I bid you a goodnight, Isadora."

Now that shit makes me stop, spin around to face him and take notice.

No one knows that name not even Benny calls me that. He knows my full name, but he also knows I prefer to be called Issy, and therefore my full name has never been mentioned.

"A kiss, and you will tell me how you know?" I ask him in disbelief.

"A kiss. Yes."

I walk back and when I reach him he looks at me waiting to see what I'll do. He's so close now I can smell him. He smells so good, like a man that knows he has it all. He smells of the ocean and damn hard work.

Before I can open my mouth, he reaches for me again and places his lips on mine, his hand holding my head in place as his tongue seeks permission to enter.

I'm letting a stranger kiss me, and I like it.

I like it, a lot.

PLAYETTE

His hand holds my pink hair in place, if he tugs on it, it will come away from my head. He doesn't, though. His other hand grips my hip and pulls me to him, so our bodies are touching.

He's...

He's...

Fuck.

He's perfect.

I pull away putting some distance between us, I need to breathe and having him that close doesn't allow me to breathe at all.

"Now, tell me?" I ask, catching my breath.

"No." My eyes go wide. "You didn't give me that kiss, I took it. The kiss I want to give you is not on those lips." His eyes travel down my legs and stops at my pussy, while his tongue darts out and licks his bottom lip like he's a starving man.

A laugh bubbles up from inside me. "You're insane," I say, shaking my head.

In one step he's back on me again, his lips hard this time as they touch mine. He pushes me back until I reach the wall, and his hands explore my thigh and he pushes up to my pussy under my skirt. He rubs his hand on the outside, making me moan into his mouth before he goes to move my G-string.

When he does, I push on his chest hard and he backs away with a smirk on his face.

"Maybe. Maybe not. But I can smell you, and I

know you want it." He sniffs his fingers and I shake my head.

The door to the club opens and Benny steps out, seeing me first.

"Good, your back. What the hell happ—" He pauses and looks directly at my stranger. Benny's back straightens and his head drops just a touch. "Sorry, sir, I didn't know you were out here. I just came to speak to Issy." My stranger watches me for a reaction. I look down at his hand and see the *red skull*.

Fuck!

How the hell did I not see that before?

How could I not have noticed he had the marking?

"Isadora, seems you have your answer."

I blanch. Looking back to Benny, he steps back, turns, and goes inside shutting the door.

"What's your name?" I ask, hoping he won't say what I think he's going to.

"Jasper."

Fuck!

Fuck!

Fuckidy fuck.

He's their leader—the one in charge of the Moretti Mafia.

I pale at his words.

"So, now you know who I am?"

I don't know exactly who he is as a person, but

PLAYETTE

what I do know is that he's nothing good. And he's my biggest target.

"You can come back to mine," I say in an attempt to make my voice sound neutral.

"You either have a thing for power, or you have an agenda, Isadora. Which one is it?" He steps closer to me again. I place my hand on his chest, careful to not let it shake so he notices.

"You owe me a kiss, do you not?" I say with as much seduction as I can muster.

"I suppose you're right." He reaches for my hand and wraps his fingers through mine. If I kill him, the power will be knocked down. I may have more of a chance with the others. This asshole, he's the one I want the most.

It's been ten years since my parents were murdered. And right now, I'm taking one of their killers to my apartment. This could be stupid, or I could get lucky. Either way, it's a chance I can't pass up.

Even if he is a killer.

"Isadora."

I don't live far, and once we pull up out the front, he waits for me open the door before he comes inside. He looks around, there's nothing personal here. It's just clothes, and more clothes and shoes littered across the carpet. It's the way I need to keep it. So, when someone comes to clean up my mess after they kill me, they won't have to worry about the poor girl with the photographs on the wall, or about the family that loved her. No, they won't have to deal with any of that.

Just clothes and shoes.

"Do I call you, Jasper?" I ask.

"You're a bit of a playette, aren't you?"

I relish in the name.

I wasn't a slut, but I didn't hold any attachments to any of the men I took to bed with me. And I have no love or even like to give anyone.

My world was torn open and everything seeped out of me—compassion, love, sympathy, pity, kindness, all of it. All out there for the world to see my pain, so why would I let them take anything else from me. My body's mine, and mine alone, to play with as I like, to do with as I please.

I first slept with someone when I was fifteen and it damn well hurt. A lot. It sucked. It was disturbing and I was affected for a while. But then the second time—I liked it, a lot.

Looking up at Jasper, I wonder how many woman he's had at his beck and call. I bet he's slept with hundreds of women in his lifetime.

He takes a seat, kicks his feet up on the table and sits back with his fingers interlinked behind his head. "Why don't you strip for me, Isadora."

PLAYETTE

"Stop saying my name like that."

"Why?"

Because he's not meant to call me that. No one calls me that!

"It's Issy."

"I prefer Isadora."

My hand touches the hem of my skirt and I pull it down with a shimmy of my hips. He watches my every move, assessing me as he does.

"Why don't *you* remove something?" I ask, putting my back to him so he now has a full view of my taut ass. Looking over my shoulder at him, I unclip my bra and let it fall to the floor.

"No, I think I won't."

Turning around I keep myself covered by my hands and step up to him.

Jasper reaches forward pulling my hands away so he can see me.

"Why not? Don't you want to play?" I ask in a soft voice.

"I haven't quite worked you out yet, Isadora. But I will. And while I'm doing so, you're not allowed to fuck any of my men. Do you understand?"

I reach for his hand and place it on my breast.

He doesn't squeeze because he's waiting for me to answer.

"You don't want to share?" I ask.

He stands, keeping his hand on my breast. "I don't share, Isadora."

I nod my head while checking with my eyes for my bag on the table, and I wonder how I can get him to take what's packed neatly inside it.

"Would you like a drink?" I ask.

He stands, towering over me. "I'll be back for you. In the meantime, you don't work at the club anymore. You don't speak to any of my men, either."

"What?" The word spits from my mouth before I can stop it. I shouldn't be arguing with him, he's where I need him to be to do what I have to do. But him commanding me, I don't like that either. I don't take well to commands, not from a man who I've dreamt of killing for so damn long.

"Do you not understand, Isadora?" He tightens his hold on my breast.

I nod. I'm a bit dumbfounded right now.

He removes his hand and lifts my chin. "I'm not a nice man, Isadora, and those who disobey me don't usually like the outcome. I have eyes and ears everywhere. Stay where you are, and be a good girl. Do you understand?"

"Why?" I ask, confused.

He reaches for my ass and pulls me against him, I feel he's so hard right now.

"You're hiding something, but I'm not sure

PLAYETTE

what it is. But I do love to solve problems, and what better way than to have you in the meantime. I like the taste of something sweet and deceiving."

His words shock me.

I step back, but he won't let me.

"Yes. See, that fear that flashed in your eyes just then. Keep it. Because I'm not what you think, Isadora, and those I take a liking to, it's usually for a reason. I've yet to find why I like you." He walks to my door, opens it, and leaves me standing there in nothing but a G-string. "I'll be back for you. Stay put."

He closes the door and I know the threat is very real.

I sit on my bed.

What the fuck just happened?

And fuck. He's just told me I can't see any of his men.

This could ruin everything I've worked so hard to achieve.

And I've endured so much to become what I think they need. What a man needs in a woman.

Fucking hell!

CHAPTER 7
Isadora

I WAIT, BECAUSE he told me to. And I have to. I don't want to lose my way in, I worked so hard for this moment, and now he may very well take it away from me.

Now, I have to regard him as my only way in, and I also have to be extra careful about it. If he knows my name, and if he's done some hard digging, he might actually find out who I am. Granted I'm under a different surname now. I changed it to be the same as my uncle's so as to gain some anonymity.

I sit on my bed waiting, and I don't do it patiently. I'm angry, angry that his simple commands I must obey. If he was a man who I wanted to sleep with, and just sleep with, you bet I would not be taking any of his commands seriously. But he isn't. He's someone who runs one of the most notorious mafias in the country. Men who kill and get away with it. He will kill me the minute he finds out who I am, and I don't think my death would even register on his regret scale nor bother the authorities due to the mafia links so firmly entrenched into their ranks.

Sharon knocks on my door, but I don't answer her. I have no respect for her, and I don't plan to help her again anytime soon.

I wait all night.

He doesn't come back.

The next night is the same.

I wait again.

He doesn't come.

By the third night, there's no way I am staying.

I head to the club. I was driving myself crazy sitting there by myself. I'm a loner by nature, but to not have anything at all to do, that's what drives me up the wall.

Benny spots me first, his eyes go wide as he makes his way over to me on fast legs. He grabs my arm and pulls me until we're near the wall. "You shouldn't be here. Jasper told me not to let you work. What have you gotten yourself into?" He touches his forehead and shakes it.

"It's all right, Benny. I just came to look and

PLAYETTE

have a drink. Not to work, I promise."

"You should go," he says.

"No. I should stay. Don't be silly." I look away from him and notice Ace and the other two guys sitting in the same spot where I met them last time.

"Don't, Issy. He isn't someone you want to piss off."

I turn to Benny. "What do you know of him?"

He scratches his face. "He's the head of the Mafia for a reason, Issy. He's ruthless. He's merciless. He's cruel. There's no remorse to his viciousness." Benny walks away thinking that's a fair warning and it is. I know he's trying to help me, and I'm appreciative of that fact. But little does he know I already understand everything about these boys and their savage intent and brutal ways.

Turning on my heels—tonight I have on a dress, a very short one, instead of the usual skirt I wear to work—I head off in the direction of the boys.

Ace spots me first, and puts out his hand for me to take. I contemplate not taking it until Ace stands and reaches for me anyway. He pulls me onto his lap, and turns me so I'm sitting right over his cock. "Pink, I've missed you."

I don't say anything.

As I spin to face him, a hand touches my arm

and pulls me up. I slam into a hard body, one with a smell I instantly recognize. I attempt to pull away, but he won't let me. Instead, he holds me to him.

"Boss, give her back. I want to play," Ace says in a whining voice.

Jasper ignores him and leans into my ear. "I warned you to stay where you were."

"I was bored," I whimper.

His hand slides down my dress until he touches my ass. "I don't give a fuck."

"Boss," Ace calls.

Jasper's hardness is pressed against me and I have trouble moving. "This one is off-limits. Don't touch her again," Jasper says into my hair, the way he said it holds a threat to his men. His touch, even if I tell myself to hate it and that he shouldn't be touching me, I definitely shouldn't desire it. The problem is I really like it, though. I'm craving his possessiveness and the way his hands touch me with power and desire, it's how I want to be touched.

"I found her first."

Jasper straightens, his hand grips tighter on my ass almost to the point of bruising. "Do you want a bullet?" he asks Ace.

I hear no response at all, as I am now pulled to sit on Jasper's lap. When I do, his hand goes between my legs not moving simply blocking

PLAYETTE

any view. I look to Ace who's now glancing down. Jasper's other hand is around my waist and he pulls me back into him. "What did you find out?" Jasper asks.

It's Carter who answers, but his voice is strained. "No sign of a struggle. It looks like he simply went to sleep and never woke up." I sit up straighter at his words. "What the fuck, boss. That can't happen, can it?"

Jasper answers, "We'll look into it."

Glancing up at Carter, he rubs his head and I feel almost sorry for him until I remember what an asshole his brother was. He deserved to die, I just wish it could have been more painful.

Turning, I see Gabe watching me, he smirks and honestly it's scary.

"You will be coming with me." I turn to face Jasper. He spoke directly in my ear, so when I do turn we come face to face.

"Will I now?"

He looks at my lips. "I always get what I want."

"And it's me you want?" I ask, leaning forward not quite touching his lips.

"Yes. You still owe me a kiss." Jasper stands, and when he does, so do all three of his men. When we start walking out, so do they. "That your friend?" Jasper points to Heather who's watching us with excitement. She smiles and offers me a simple wave. I don't answer, but he takes that as an answer. "Benny, we will take the smiling one, too."

Benny groans and walks over to Heather, says something to her, which makes her eyes sparkle even more. My heart drops to my feet thinking she's coming with us, and to that house. If they know she means something to me, if this somehow goes wrong they will kill her without even blinking. I take a deep breath as I look her way and try to think of a reason, some sort of excuse to get her out of it but nothing comes to mind.

She prances over to Ace, and he grabs hold of her waist.

I watch and Ace smiles at me. "Do you care, pink?" Ace asks me.

Jasper grunts next and I turn back to look at him. "Do you?" I shake my head. "I'll tell him to be gentle with her, if you're good."

I knew the world I was destined to enter wouldn't be all rainbows and pretty colors. These boys own this town, they kill, which they do easily and not one of them has been locked up for their actions. They are excellent in covering their tracks and leaving no trace behind. They're essentially their own gods. Businesses pay them commission for keeping them safe, that is if they don't they take their businesses away from them first.

PLAYETTE

You don't fuck with the Moretti Mafia, they fuck with you, and they don't care how much.

"You will be taking that silly wig off, too," Jasper says as we step outside, the cold air hits my skin and I shiver. The guys slide into their own car while we slip into Jasper's.

"Where have you been?" I ask as he presses the ignition and it starts the car. Jasper pulls out and I already know where he's going—to that mansion. My bag sits on my lap with my baggie inside. And it's making me all kinds of elated, but also trepidation is raging inside me. I plan to use it again tonight.

On him? I'm not sure.

"I've been digging, we lost one of our own recently." He turns to look at me.

"I was there," I say referring to the night they found him.

Jasper changes gears in the car, and honestly, it's damn hot watching him.

"I heard. Why were you there?" he asks, dropping down a gear.

"Ace took me."

"Are you a whore, Isadora?"

Fucking hell, he doesn't mince his damn words.

"Do you want me to be a whore?"

He smirks pulling into the driveway I remember, but he doesn't stop out the front like everyone else does. Instead, he continues around the back to a smaller house. That's where he stops and gets out, walks around to my door and opens it for me, offering me a hand and I take it stepping out.

"I haven't made up my mind yet. I fuck with whores all the time, Isadora, but you're different."

"How so?" I ask.

Jasper pushes on me as I come to a full standing position. His hand comes up and tugs at my wig. "Lose this. Now."

I do as he says, pulling it from my head, and unclipping my long hair, letting it drop down my back. He hasn't seen my hair without my wig. He picks up a few strands of my soft hair and lets it drop back down. His eyes, ever so light, find mine. "Now I see *you*. Tell me, Isadora, how much more are you hiding from me?"

I look past him to the house, where I know Heather is. I don't want to leave her alone in that place by herself. I've seen the bruises on some of the girls, and I don't want her to be like them. She's the weak link I never wanted. Yet, she's there on my conscience. And instead of focusing on smooching the big boss, I'm now worried about her.

Turning back to Jasper, I smile. "Wouldn't you like to know."

He looks behind him, then back to me. "A drink, so you can see your friend, then you're

PLAYETTE

mine."

I sigh in relief.

Jasper takes my hand, threads my fingers in his and pulls me to the back door which is open. "There she is." He points to her. Heather's seated by herself, a drink in her hand as she looks around. When she spots me she runs over almost tackling me, but Jasper doesn't let go of my hand.

"They want me to go for a swim, but one of the girls pushed me away, so I don't know what to do. What are you up to?" She looks from me to Jasper.

"You should go home," I say to her, but she shakes her head.

"I just got here."

"You should go home, Heather," I say in sterner, firmer voice.

"What your friend is trying to say is… why don't you go grab yourself another drink, and have some fun. She'll be occupied for a while."

"Can I come with you?" she asks. Her doe eyes are begging me.

"Go home, Heather."

Jasper pulls me to him, and she notices.

"I'll go for a swim."

I shake my head slowly as Jasper hands me a drink. "Go. Have fun. Isadora is coming with me."

"Isadora?" she asks, confusion is littered on

her face as the small lines crease above her eyebrows.

"Goodnight Heather," I say, turning to walk out the same way we came in.

He's silent until we pass his car, and get to the front door of the second smaller house.

"You're protective of her." He turns and taps my nose. "I like to know your weaknesses. You don't tell me much, but you express a lot in your face. Did you know that? It gives you away. Provides me with so much information."

I did, and I've tried to rectify it, but it never seems to work. So, I've learned to make excuses for it instead.

"And will you tell me yours?" I ask stepping up so our bodies are aligned and touching. "All your secrets? You must have plenty. What are you again? The boss?" My fingers touch his lips, drawing an outline.

He bites at my finger, putting it between his lips then sucking before releasing it. Why are you asking Isadora?"

"You know all mine, why can't I know yours?" I smirk as he steps away, opens the door to his house, and I follow him inside. It's open plan living. There are two single suede black sofas then a white two-seater next to that. No television just a fireplace with a small coffee table and a few magazines scattered over the top.

PLAYETTE

"But I don't believe I do know them all. Now do I?" Jasper walks to the very open and huge kitchen. Black large lights hang from the ceiling as he grabs two shot glasses and pours tequila into each one. He eyes me over his lashes, waiting for my reply.

"A girl has to have a few secrets, now doesn't she?"

He picks up the shot glasses and walks over to me, handing me one.

"You should stop wearing that wig, it does nothing for you."

"But I like it."

"You're beautiful, Isadora. But you know that already, don't you?"

I smile at his words and he smiles back, and as he does a snake comes to mind. He slithers close to his prey so he can strike. And let's face it, close is where he is right now.

I drink the tequila in one go clutching the glass in my hand, and I lean forward to taste his lips. He lets me, he tastes of tequila and mint. Jasper doesn't touch me when he kisses me, his mouth does all the work, and because he's so good at that he doesn't need hands to seduce me.

I'm excited to fuck him.

I bet he'll be great, probably one of the best I've ever had.

Pulling away, I lick my lips.

He puts his glass to his lips and finishes his drink. With a smirk he looks at me. "I'm onto you, Isadora Marine, but that's okay. I like to bite."

CHAPTER 8
Isadora

JASPER DIRECTS ME to a room where he turns on the light and starts unbuttoning his shirt, kicks off each shoe, then turns to me with the front open. His chest is covered in ink, dark black ink. He smirks when he sees me ogling. He pulls the shirt off his shoulders followed by his belt, that doesn't get dropped to the floor. Instead, he wraps it around his hand as the smirk never leaves his mouth.

"What is it you want, Isadora?" he asks me.

I want him.

I want what only he can give me.

He's a bad boy, so I'm hoping hard, fast and

rough.

I should be nervous to be in this situation with him, but I'm not.

"It's you that wants me here, Jasper. Why don't you tell me what you want from me?"

He quirks an eyebrow. "That game?" he asks.

I'm not sure if I want to play a game with him, I have this funny feeling Jasper will never lose. "What is it you want to do to me, Jasper?"

"I want to taste you first. Take that skirt off and lay on the bed, put your hands behind your head and spread your legs. You owe me a kiss after all."

The belt tightens in his fist as my hands touch the edge of my skirt pulling it down. When it drops to the floor, I leave my G-string on, and climb onto his bed lying on my back and turning to face him then placing my hands above my head with a smile.

Jasper walks over, my hands go back and the belt comes free as he grips them and starts to wrap it firmly around them tying me to the post of the bed. When he's done, he steps back, smiles and admires his handiwork and stalks by stepping to the end of the bed, then to the other side of the bed, eyeing my body as he goes.

No words are spoken, I guess none are needed.

His shirt that was caught on his wrists comes

PLAYETTE

free, and the amount of artwork covering his skin makes me gasp. He's absolutely covered. There's not one small patch of skin available. When he sees my eyes roaming up and down, he smiles.

"Is that surprise or interest you have on your face?" he asks me.

"A bit of both," I answer truthfully.

"The ink all holds meaning. Do you want to know what they stand for?" I nod and watch him as he points to the large one on his chest. "This is my grandfather's symbol, my father's, and now mine. You know who we are, I know you do. You play the whore role, but I see it in your eyes that something else is there."

I don't answer, it's best not to.

He moves away from the large crest and smirks when he gets to a woman's face. "This was my mother. I killed her with my bare hands. She was such a beautiful woman, wasn't she?" My eyes go wide at his words. "Oh, yes, I can see by that crinkled forehead that you didn't expect that." He drops a knee between my feet and looks at me. "You let a snake wrap around you and expect to not be eaten?" he asks, leaning his head to the side.

What have I gotten myself into? Jesus! Fuck.

"I see shock in your eyes, Isadora. Is it the snake comment?"

"How did you know?"

"You whispered it when I pulled away from our kiss, I bet you didn't even know."

I didn't. I'm positive I thought it, but never uttered the words.

His hand touches my face and he strokes my cheek. "What do you want, Isadora?" His fingers leave my face, and he slides them between us until he cups my sex. "I want a lot of things, but in this life, I am a patient man." He leans down and kisses my lips. "Now tell me, Isadora, what is it that you want? Is it my tongue between your legs?" I nod my head as he moves my G-string to the side. "Words Isadora, I like words."

"Yes."

"Good girl." He slides down kissing my stomach as he goes, until he reaches the top of my G-string. He slides it down, and I lift to accommodate him, as he pulls it off my body with a sly smile.

"How many girls do you bring here?" I ask while watching his every move.

"Wouldn't you like to know?" He winks then drops his head between my legs, the first swipe has me dropping my head back, and my hands gripping onto the belt holding me in place. The second stroke of his tongue has me yearning for more, much more.

I start to squirm, I can't help it. The way he moves and touches me with his tongue is something I've never experienced before. Only

PLAYETTE

two guys have gone down on me, and neither of them made me feel this way. He hits all the right spots, and when he does my grip becomes a little tighter to hopefully help stop the moan that wants to leave my mouth.

When I start thrusting my hips, he holds me in place so I can't move, and it's damn torture. So much fucking torture. But the best kind.

He slips in a finger while his tongue works magic on my clit, and when he does, he pushes in hard making me want to meet him thrust for thrust. His tongue drops from my clit to where his fingers are and he licks around, then back up. It's only moments after that my breathing becomes heavy and I feel myself building.

My pussy starts to clench, and my hands grip to the point that when I look back at them they're red from holding on so tightly.

"Fuckkk," is all that manages to leave my mouth.

Jasper keeps pushing in, his tongue not stopping its dance on my sensitive clit as he fucks me with his mouth.

I'm one of the lucky girls who can come through vaginal penetration, but clit stimulation is something else and fuck me, Jasper sure as shit knows what he's doing.

Pity, I have to kill him.

He would be good to keep around.

I like him.

But secretly, I detest him and what he stands for, and more than that, he has no idea.

I want him dead, but I also want him between my legs.

He's playing a war with my body and my mind. *What will win?*

Jasper pulls away when my body is spent. My breathing slows, and my lip is now sore from biting it to keep myself from screaming.

I have a filthy mouth when I come, every possible expletive leaves my mouth, and I'm proud of myself tonight that I didn't let that happen.

Jasper sits up still dressed in his trousers as he looks down at me. "You taste as sweet as I imagined." He licks his fingers while smirking at me. I watch him, my breathing slowly coming back to normal and I pull on the restraints.

"Oh yes, that... I don't like to be touched." Jasper gets up and when he does I see his back. It's full of scars. Every inch of his back is red with raised scars, some are old, but there's also some new ones.

I gasp, and he turns back to me.

"No touching, as I said." He walks over, his cock hard and in my face through his trousers as he undoes the belt on the bed. When my hands are free I rub my wrists, they're bright red from being pulled on.

PLAYETTE

A knock comes on the door and I pull up the sheet.

"Yes."

The door opens and Gabe steps in, he quickly looks my way then back to Jasper. You're needed." He nods then leaves.

Jasper turns back to me, reaching for his shirt and sliding it on over his body. My eyes roam him and despite the scars and tattoos he's fit, has abs and the most beautiful shoulders.

"You stay and wait for me. I'll be a few hours."

I sit up. "What if I don't want to?"

He climbs on the bed, his shirt still open as he comes close to my lips nipping at them with his teeth. "You'll do what's best for you, and I think you know what's best for you." He stares and I nod my head. "You can go see your friend if you wish, but be in my bed when I get back."

"Are you keeping me?" I ask, kicking the sheet off me and standing.

He's at the door now, but stops before he opens it to look back at me. "The things I keep don't usually survive. You don't want to be kept by me, Isadora." He steps off, leaving me standing there with my mouth semi-open.

What the fuck.

The minute he's gone, I reach for my bag and check that everything's still in place. When I slide my hand into the side compartment, which is full of tampons and pads—a great deterrent for snooping people—I feel for what I'm after and smile when my hand comes into direct contact with the baggie.

Taking my bag, I go back to the main house and spot Heather straight away sitting near, what I guess, is their dance floor.

She notices me and sits up straighter. "Where have you been?" She pulls on my arm, so I have to bend to her height.

"Busy."

"I bet you were," she says with a devilish smile.

"I told you to go home, Heather."

She looks around then back to me. "I didn't want to, it's nice here."

Arrrgggghhh, for fuck's sake. I reach for my keys to my shitty place and hand them over to her.

"Go to mine then, I won't be back until the morning."

"Are you staying with him?" she asks, standing.

"Yes. Now go home, and don't come back here."

Heather looks past my shoulder. "He went to get me a drink, though." She nods.

Turning, I see one of the members. The one who was fucking the two girls last night while smirking at me. I take the drink from his hand and smile. "Thanks."

PLAYETTE

He looks me over then behind me to Heather. "You want to join in, hot stuff? I love me more than one bird at a time." I cringe at his words and so badly want to raise my lip in disgust at the way he speaks, but I restrain myself. Bird, who the fuck calls a woman that now anyway? What does he think he is, someone from England?

"Oh no, she's bleeding. So she's going home." I smile at him.

Heather takes a deep breath, and when I turn my back to this guy to face Heather I mouth 'home' to her. She nods, and turns to walk off. Hands slide around my waist to touch me. I pull back and clink our drinks together. "Cheers." I drink it all, as does he.

"Let me get you another one before we head up." I smirk up at him.

He nods his head eagerly and adjusts his cock through his jeans. *Disgusting.*

Walking away, I reach the fridge, grab two bottles of beer and slide them on the counter, I stealthily grab the baggie and pour a small amount of its contents into his drink without the disgusting ass noticing. Taking a sip of mine, I turn around to see Gabe standing there. Watching me.

Fuck! How much did he see?

My heart starts racing as I manage a fake a smile. He reaches for the drink I'm not drinking and takes it from my hand. My palms are now sweaty, and my heart feels like it's about to beat out of my chest.

"You were in the boss' room?"

I nod while he watches me.

He lifts the bottle to his mouth, and before he can take a sip the guy who I went to get the beer for hits Gabe on the arm. "That's mine..." he snaps the bottle and nods his head to me, "... and that's mine, too."

Gabe shakes his head. "She's with the boss, no touching."

"Fuck!" he whines and turns around, taking the drink with him.

"Why do you look so pale?" Averting my eyes, I look back to Gabe who's spoken to me.

"I thought I saw someone I knew," I lie.

"Not here you won't. Now why don't you go back to your room before you get yourself into a *lot* of trouble?"

I nod my head and turn, walking out.

Except, I don't go back to the room. Instead, I head around the side to where there's a massive infinity pool and dive in.

Fuck.

CHAPTER 9
Jasper

"WHAT DO YOU plan to do with her?" Carter asks standing next to me as I look down from his room to see her swimming. She does several laps effortlessly as if she was made for an Olympic team. Her body's fit. I know she has stamina but I guess I didn't realize how much.

"Fuck, does she stop?" he asks five minutes into watching her.

She hasn't stopped swimming laps since we've been watching Isadora.

"So far, I'm enjoying her."

Carter shakes his head at my words. "You fuck them and get rid of them. Why is she still here?"

he asks.

I grind my teeth together. "Do you want her, Carter?"

That would really piss me off, and he knows it. She has me all fucked-up, and I have no damn reason why. So, my best bet is to keep her where I can find her. Have her within touching distance at all times. Until I figure out what she is to me. Who she is to me.

He raises his hands in the air. "No, boss. But one has to wonder why you're keeping her."

"She amuses me. I haven't quite figured her out yet."

"I didn't know you wanted to figure her out."

I take a deep breath at his words and remember that I actually like him, that I shouldn't kill him for asking me one hundred and one fucking stupid questions. And he's also right, I've never cared enough to figure out a woman before. *So why her?*

"Boss."

Turning around, Gabe's standing in the doorway his eyes wild. "Shawn's fucking dead."

"What?" I ask, confused.

"He's dead, boss. Just found him on the sofa. Dead."

"Why the fuck are my people dying?" I ask, more to myself than anyone who's around me. This can't be happening, not in my house of all

PLAYETTE

places. Someone's got balls of steel to kill in my territory, and they won't like the outcome when I find them. Turning around to Gabe I order, "Get everyone out of here. No more fucking parties until we get this shit sorted."

Gabe nods his head and turns to leave, but stops when I say his name. "Not her, though. Leave her where she is. Put a few guys around her."

He nods and walks off. Gabe works fast. Within seconds of him leaving, I turn around and watch as the back door swings open and two burly security guys walk out, one standing on either side of the pool while Isadora continues to swim. She doesn't even bother to look up to see what's happening around her.

"We've been having trouble with a real estate tycoon in Evergreen. How do you want to handle him?" Carter asks.

"What's his name?"

"Gunner Reid."

I smile at that name, I know of him. If you're smart, you know who he is and you keep on top of him. Not only is he dangerous, he's also one of the smartest businessmen alive.

"Call him over for a visit. Tell him it's a personal invitation… from me."

Carter nods and walks out, shutting the door behind him while I stay where I am watching her.

Isadora swims a few more laps before she finally looks up and when she does she stops moving and her body locks tight.

"Who are you?" Security doesn't answer. Isadora looks around then back to my men. "Can I keep swimming?" Again, they don't answer. So, she spins onto her back, her perfect fake tits sitting flawlessly on her chest as she floats. Luckily for her they're covered otherwise my men would be having their eyes removed, personally by me.

Turning my back on her, I step down the stairs to my men. Carter and Gabe are talking animatedly and stop once I reach them. I had eight of my most trusted men working alongside me, now I have six. That's two dead in a matter of days. There's a damn issue and I need to get to the bottom of whatever the fuck's going on.

"Same death, boss. No sign of struggle. Simply looks like he went to sleep with his eyes wide open."

Fuck.

"Send them both to the closest morgue. Pay whatever they need to do a thorough autopsy. I want them tested for toxins, fucking poison, and whatever else they need to test for. Fucking get to it, now!"

"Boss." I turn to Carter who's stopped me from heading out to my house. "Don't you think you should take her home, and stay and wait for

PLAYETTE

Gunner Reid to arrive?"

"No. Make him wait." I continue walking outside and into the yard. Isadora's still floating on her back in the crystal clear pool when I reach her.

"Are the bodyguards absolutely necessary?" she asks while her eyes remain transfixed on the sky.

"They're a necessity."

"If you say so."

I strip my clothes and dive into the water. Swimming over to meet her, she stays on her back until my hands reach out to pull her to me.

"I do. Now tell me…. did you behave when I was gone?" Her hair's floating around us, and her lips are soft and pink. I want to taste her again, claim her lips, and fuck her so hard she'll be dreaming of me for weeks.

"I always behave unless instructed otherwise." She winks, her arms wrap around my shoulders as she drops her head back to float, all the time being careful to not lay her hands on my back. Her body is flush against mine. She's wearing a G-string and I can feel her bare ass against my fingers.

"I find that hard to believe."

Isadora smiles, looking up at the night sky.

I drag a finger down her neck until I reach between her breasts. "You're hiding something.

I'm not sure what, but I'm eager to figure it out. I like a good puzzle."

"A girl has to have some secrets." She pulls her head out of the water and places a teasing kiss on my lips.

"So, you've said."

"Boss." Ace walks out.

Isadora tenses while I hold her.

"Gunner Reid's on his way. ETA... ten minutes."

"Occupy him."

"Yes, sir."

Ace doesn't even notice Isadora, and I feel her relax when he walks away.

"Do you like him?" I ask, waiting for her to show me any sign that she's lying.

"Yes." She tells me the truth.

"Would you rather be in there with him than here with me?"

She shakes her head in answer. I like that answer and lean forward, cupping her face with my large hand and kiss her lips. She kisses me back, and when she pulls away, I let her go. Isadora floats on the surface of the water again, clearly she's totally relaxed.

"How long am I expected to stay here, Jasper?" she asks, her eyes directed to the night sky.

"You can leave if you want, but I'll find you.

PLAYETTE

So, don't hide."

"And can I go back to work?" she asks.

"If you wish."

Isadora smiles as she comes to a stand, then swims to the edge before she climbs out elegantly. Her perfect ass is on display, and then she looks over her shoulder as the doors open, and Gunner Reid's standing there. His eyebrows are pulled together tightly and his lips are in a thin line. Normally, he wouldn't be welcome in my home, especially with everything that's happening, but Gunner is one of the smartest men I know. He lives and works a different county, Evergreen. We don't see him. He stays on his side and I stay on mine. Although, slowly but surely I haven't failed to notice him buying up property in the Moretti Mafia area. He just doesn't realize yet, that I know. One thing about Gunner, he doesn't like being made to wait, and that fact is clearly evident on his face.

"You can leave now," I dismiss while she pauses and looks his way.

Gunner's the opposite of everything I am. He has curly hair, no tattoos, and is a Greek god. Women go crazy to simply know him, even though he holds some of the biggest demons known to mankind.

"Jasper," he states, looking from Isadora to me. If he wanted her, he could probably have her, but that doesn't mean I wouldn't kill him for trying. I would. No one can have her until I figure out exactly where I want her.

"You don't want to play?" Her long hair is being twirled between her elegant fingers. "I do like to play, Jasper." Isadora bats her eyes enticingly.

As I step out of the pool I'm shaking my head, and when I turn to look at her she is watching me, not Gunner.

"Go. Now, Isadora."

She curtsies. "As you wish." She twirls, bare ass and all, as she steps inside my home, not the mansion. I wait until the front door shuts before I slide on my shirt, and turn back to face Gunner whose hands are in his pockets as he watches me.

"We have business to discuss! Land you are *attempting* to stop us from acquiring," I ask. He wants it as well, so he's fighting me for it.

He simply nods once, then he fires back, "You don't own it. Much like you don't own the storefront located on it."

"And you do?"

"No." He smirks. "Indeed, I don't. But I do know who does."

"Their daughter was never killed, Jasper. She owns it."

"Where the fuck is she?" Gunner taps his foot impatiently.

PLAYETTE

"Isn't that your job… to know *your* town?"

I step closer. "Do you run yours?" I ask inquisitively, but also trying to get a rise from him.

He smirks. "Not yet, but I will. I'm a patient man, Jasper. Can you say the same?"

"Give me *all* the details you have on that land." I know he has it, and saves me looking into it when it's easily obtainable through him. Gunner never goes into anything unless he knows every single solitary detail.

"Already have it. Now, next time you call a meeting with me, it better be more enjoyable than this bullshit. Do you understand?"

I nod, taking the paperwork from his hand as he leaves.

"And Jasper?" He stops at the door. "I'd watch that one if I was you." He smirks before he spins to walk away, but I can see the cunningness shine through his features, and in the way he skillfully deceives.

CHAPTER 10
Isadora

I LEFT THE minute I could. I wasn't planning on staying longer than necessary that's for sure.

Stepping out of the shower the next day, I spray myself with a scent that honestly smells like vanilla cupcakes and dress in my normal attire getting ready for my shift.

Walking into the club for my shift, I spot Benny who looks older than he did a few days ago. *What the hell is going on?* He looks tired maybe, or perhaps there's something else happening.

Benny walks straight over to me and grabs my arm. "I can't keep up. They want you to work then they don't. Which fucking one is it?"

"I'm all yours tonight, Benny."

With a loud huff, he lets me go. "Look, I don't want you in here tonight if they decide to come in. The girls are complaining, and you need a break. I need you to deliver something instead."

"Sure, if I get to use your car."

Benny rolls his eyes. "It's in Evergreen. Gunner Reid's expecting payment, and Jasper asked me to deliver to him. You can do it because clearly, I have enough shit going on in here right now." He pushes an envelope into my hand and then a card. "That's the address. Don't fucking linger. Pass it on. And leave."

"What's it for?" I ask looking at the envelope knowing its money.

"None of your business. Got it?" he huffs at me.

"Yes, boss," I say, smiling.

"And put on a damn coat, or change, or something, but don't go dressed like that," he says, waving a hand down my front.

Heading out the back to where my clothing and other personal items are located, I slide out of my skirt into a pair of tight-fitting denim jeans. As I pull the cloth over my legs it feels good to be wearing them again, it's been too long.

"You didn't come back," Heather says, surprising me.

"I stayed longer than expected."

PLAYETTE

"I slept, then I left, I hope that's okay?"

I give her a simple nod in answer to her question, nothing at my place holds anything of value or importance. I don't want to go into details with her, she needs to keep her nose clean. I feel like I have to protect her and I have no idea why, but somehow she crept in and I didn't realize until she'd already embedded herself in my soul.

After I left Jasper's last night I went straight to my uncle's place and told him about number two. He showed real signs of enjoyment, but it was a fleeting emotion and was gone no sooner than it came.

"Of course, Heather. Go there tonight, if you want. I'll just be chilling."

"You aren't working tonight?" she asks while looking me up and down.

"No, I'm on an errand." I lean in and kiss her cheek before I grab my bag and step out the back into an alleyway where Benny's car is located. It's a nice Mercedes, and I've never driven one before. Getting in, I smile wide while turning the key-less ignition and starting the engine. This feels so much better than the shit cars my uncle made me test drive to get my license when growing up.

It doesn't take me long once I'm out on the highway to arrive in Evergreen, and once I'm there the car's navigation system directs me to the address where a stunning high-rise apartment complex sits in front of me. All I can see is glass from about the first floor up to the obvious penthouse suites located on the top floors. With steel support beams and gorgeous balconies, this building is stunning.

Walking inside the foyer, I'm met with a bank of elevators. Taking the elevator to the top floor, I'm honestly surprised by the lack of security. Stepping out, I walk the short distance to the door and press the bell. It's late, but all the lights are on. When the door is opened I'm met with Gunner Reid, who I just so happened to do some research on after I left Jasper. He's a real estate tycoon and this is one of his many places. Smiling at him, he doesn't smile back, but he sure as shit looks me over. Then his eyes stop on what's in my hand and he reaches for it.

"Benny sent me," I tell him.

"Figured as much."

A girl walks behind him. I'm shocked to see the sheer amount of bruises covering her body, then there's another. My eyes go wide and he smirks. *The bastard.*

"They..." he trails off.

I look at his hand and notice he doesn't have the symbol tattoo.

So, why was... no. I shake my head.

PLAYETTE

Those girls are up and walking around, not looking like they were just beaten. Right?

"Now unless you want to join…" he trails off again, but the innuendo speaks for itself.

I look up at his eyes, if eyes could tell stories his would tell a thousand.

Danger, proceed with caution…

You want me? This will be the price you pay…

Oh, hell, no.

So, I take a step back, I already have one devil to deal with and I simply don't need another one.

"Goodnight, Isadora Marine. My best bet is you run before he figures out who you are." Fucking hell, that smile, it's manic, like full Hollywood creepy movie scary.

"Y-you k-kn…" I don't finish but he nods at my stuttering words.

"Yes, I know. But you see… he *isn't* my friend. I don't have friends, they only get in the way. He's a business acquaintance. So, as long as he lives your secret is safe with me. Well, for now, anyway."

I nod, stepping backward.

"Watch your uncle though, Isadora. Sometimes a wolf has a hard time letting go, and might just blow all you've been working toward." He shuts the door on me, and I simply stare ahead having no idea what I just walked in on, let alone what he's divulged to me.

Who the hell is that man, and how the hell does he know anything about me? I've been so secretive, so extremely careful, so I honestly have no idea.

Immediately I start searching his name on my phone again, hoping to find something before I step into the elevator, and this is the first thing that pops up.

Gunner Reid
Evergreen Real Estate
Tycoon, and most eligible bachelor.

I already knew all this, so I keep on searching and reading.

> Gunner Reid is reported to be dangerous in the business world. Not many people go against him, and those that have always seem to lose. He uncovers their secrets, some that not even trained private investigators can find. He's a man of few words, and someone you should tread lightly around.

My hands start sweating, and I'm afraid any second now I will drop my phone. Then it starts ringing, while music is blaring from his apartment.

I stare at the door thinking, *Is he going to open the door and tell me he's just told Jasper everything?*

But he can't know everything. *Can he?*

PLAYETTE

How could he possibly know everything? We've been so prudent and attentive to all the details which keep my uncle and I safe.

The phone starts ringing, stops, and then rings again. I put it to my ear and listen, waiting for whoever it is to begin speaking.

"Issy. Fuck! Are you lost?"

"No," I reply sharply to Benny while looking back at the door before spinning around and walking away to make my way to the parking garage. I drive off and out into the pouring rain, the wipers of the car finding it hard to keep up and clean the windshield effectively.

"You haven't broken my damn car, have you?" he whines.

"No," I reply.

"Thank God. You do know how much that thing cost me, right?"

"Benny, I'm on my way back."

"Good. They're asking for you again." He hangs up and my hands grab the steering wheel almost gripping it too tightly, wondering if I should simply drive away to a normal life, one that isn't so fucked-up.

I'm sure that's what my parents would have wanted for me.

Yet, here I am, avenging their deaths.

And planning to take everyone down with me.

The rain follows me back, it's a little less persistent but still teaming down by the time I reach the club. Parking Benny's car, I run to the front door and step inside. I spot them all straight away. Jasper's clearly the king of the group, he's sitting while they all stand around him, listening to his words intently.

I wonder why I never noticed him before. *Did he ever come in? Or was he always lurking around out the front?*

"Oh, thank you, God." Benny takes the keys from my hand. "I was worried."

"I'm fine. No need to worry, Benny."

He looks up at me and shakes his head, then he turns in the same direction I'm staring. "I can sneak you out, if you want?" As he's saying it Jasper turns around and looks at me. "Too late," he says, but I still hear him.

"Did they used to come in this often?" I ask Benny as Jasper stands. His men follow his line of sight straight to me. I don't have my wig on right now, and Ace doesn't look long before he turns away.

"No. They would come in for girls, but not him. Never him."

Before Jasper reaches us, Benny turns and leaves.

Jasper's cold hands touch my bare belly. My shirt is high and shows off my midriff where I'm still wet from the teaming rain outside. "Where

PLAYETTE

were you?"

"Delivery."

Jasper raises an eyebrow and I don't tell him any more than that. If that man, Gunner, knows more than Jasper, I need to keep it that way.

"Why are you here, Jasper?"

Jasper looks around. "I told you I'd come back for you."

I nod my head. "You did, but so soon?" I question with a smile.

"It seems I need to get you out of my system, and the only way to do that is to have you. So, what do you say, Isadora?" He steps in my space, his hand lays firmly on my hip. "Can I have you?"

"I'm not for sale," I say, grinning.

"Everything has a price, Isadora, even you. Tell me yours?"

I look over his shoulder, watching his men walk up to us. I pause, waiting, and then lean in and whisper, "What if I don't want you?" I purposely look past him to Ace.

Ace stands there having no idea what's going on. But I feel Jasper's grip tighten on my hip almost to the point of pain where he's about to bruise me.

My lines with him are becoming blurry, I want him, but I have things I need to do. Which would ruin my want for him. Let's face it, he will kill me.

T. L. SMITH

"Is there someone else you want?" Following my line of sight he smirks when he looks back to me. "You want one of my men?" He shakes his head. "No can do. I don't share that way."

I shrug, and Ace looks at me with a smirk. "Pink."

I smile brightly. Actually, I like him. Just not in the way I'm making Jasper believe. I have to ruffle his feathers somehow, and I can't tell him about Gunner, so this is my best option right now.

His fingers dig in further, and even though I feel the pressure I don't move away from him. Instead, I stay perfectly still.

"It's best you don't talk to her," Jasper states while staring at me.

"Oh... is this her?" Ace questions, raising an eyebrow like it's finally registering. "Almost didn't recognize you without your pink hair, pink."

I wink at him. "I prefer the pink."

"I don't. So don't wear it again," Jasper barks next to me.

"So controlling," I whine. I notice he lets me touch his shoulder when we're this close, usually I'm only allowed when his lips are locked on mine. *So, why did he tie me up last time?* He made it perfectly clear he doesn't like to be touched, so I'm careful where I place my hands. Seems it's okay on his shoulders, but he still tenses.

PLAYETTE

"Why don't you show me why you get to keep me all to yourself then?"

"Don't tease me, Isadora. I'm not a man you want to play games with."

"I have things I want to do tonight. So, I can't go with you anyway." I pull away from him and Jasper attempts to reach for me but I shake my head. "Goodnight Jasper, enjoy your night." I turn, not looking back, as I head outside. The rain is still heavy but I'm already wet, so it doesn't stop me.

"Isadora…" My name is called, so I stop and turn around. Jasper walks over to me, his chocolate hair slicking down with water and sticking to his face. He looks like sex, right now. He is sex.

"I'm going home, Jasper. Tonight you don't get to tell me what to do." I turn but he reaches for my hand pulling me back, so I have to face him.

"Women don't tell me what they want to do. They fucking listen. But you're new to my world, so I'll let that slide. This time…" he pauses, "… but that won't happen again, Isadora. You want to be in it, I know you do. You wouldn't have followed Ace, otherwise. So now, your mine. If you touch another man I will have to kill him. Do you want that? Me to kill another man because of you?" He's menacing, I see the anger etched all over his face to his eyes that hold something so sinister right now.

"What about if I touch, Ace?" I stir him a little, he damn well deserves it. Jasper pulls me to him so our bodies are touching everywhere, while the rain washes over us. Being touched by him does things to me that shouldn't happen. His touch ignites me and I don't like it, but I secretly love it.

"I'll kill him, too. Everyone's replaceable. I learned that at a young age. Even someone as significant as a mother can be replaced. What makes you think my men and women can't either?"

Fuck! I try to hold the shiver that wracks through my body at the sound of those words. He smirks and leans in, kissing my lips. I let him. One... because he's a good kisser, and two... because I'm a little afraid of him, and three... well fuck, because I like it when he kisses me. Anywhere on my body. He's a damn fine kisser.

He pulls back, and I keep my eyes closed for a second longer smiling when I look up at him.

"Don't disappoint me, Isadora. I would hate to have to hurt you, or anyone else around you." He lets me go and turns to walk off. My hands begin to shake when he's no longer touching me, my nerves are shot and my head is all over the place.

I watch his gorgeous body step back inside the club, and it isn't until the door shuts and the rain becomes heavier that I turn to leave. Wondering what tomorrow will bring.

CHAPTER 11
Jasper

"Y‍OU'RE TO STAY away from her. Do you fucking understand?" I tell Ace with a glare that could melt ice, somehow she has grown on me and the thought of another man touching her makes me so angry that I could kill whoever thinks about it. He simply stares at me. "Ace," I say, demanding he answer me.

"Fine! I found her first, you know. You stole her." He waves his hands in the air, shaking his head as he walks away.

"Boss, it's time." Gabe hands me my pistol and I holster it as we leave the house. "Two men. One's out the back the other in front." I give a curt nod as the car takes off. "It's over one-hundred thousand now, too, boss," Gabe fills me in as he reads from his iPad.

"Who let the debt get that bad?" I ask him. Small business owners aren't allowed to be in debt to that extent, especially when he already owes me his life to begin with.

"You," he says putting the iPad away.

I look to him and he casts his eyes down. "How?"

"We warned you last month that he was borrowing against the business."

"Of course, he was," I moan sitting back.

If I had a choice in the world of what my life would be like, this wouldn't be it. I was born into this world, so it's all I know. But this is not what I would choose. I do this because I was raised, groomed and coached for this, not because I choose to do it.

Despite not wanting this life, this is the life I was given, so I live it the best I can. Yes, that comes with harder days than the rest, and some things need a show of power to evoke fear to earn respect more than others. My father was feared for so much worse than me, I am not like him.

The car comes to a stop out the front of a small delivery center. Robert helps us ship drugs and launder money. Now he'll be useless to me, and I'll have to find a replacement. *Fuck.*

"Where's Robert? Back or front?" I ask Gabe.

PLAYETTE

He simply nods his head to the front.

"Go through the back entrance and secure his son," I tell him as we get out.

Carter walks in with me while Gabe and Ace slip out back.

It's quiet, the shops on this street are closed. Opening the front door I spot Richard straight away counting the cash behind the till, he spots us and freezes. His eyes look everywhere, and I see the exact moment he knows what we're here for. He runs, straight out the back. I begin looking around the shop for things I can use, but there's nothing of value. I drop a package on the floor and hear it clunk. When I bend down to retrieve it, Richard's being escorted back inside. Tim, one of my men, has him around the throat and Richard's son is in Gabe's hands.

"You want to run from me, Richard?"

"No, sir. No." He shakes his head and Tim lets him go. Richard drops to his knees in front of me and shakes his head, his hands in a prayer position as he speaks. "Please. Please, give me more time."

"You had time, Richard. Plenty of it."

"What did you do, Papa?" his son asks, looking at his father with a scrunched-up forehead.

Richard ignores him and looks at me with pleading eyes. "Just give me time, more time."

I shake my head. "Time is not something I'm willing to give. You've had enough time."

"Let me pay you back. What does he owe you?" the son asks. He's young but not young enough that he doesn't understand why we're here. I would say he's in his early twenties.

I tell him, his face pales.

He looks to his father. "How could you do that? This was Grandad's shop, and it was meant to go to me. How could you do that?"

Richard stands, faces his son. "I spent all your money, you have none. You're blind to it all, Donald. I've been taking money from this man for quite some time, and now this business is his."

"No, this is mine."

Richard shakes his head at his son, he looks past him and I can't believe what I see, he runs. Not caring about his son, leaving him behind.

"Donald, I wouldn't look if I was you." I raise the gun and in the second it takes to reach for the handle to make a run for it, my gun is raised and I pull the trigger. Richard falls, smashes into the door before sliding to the floor leaving a trail of blood behind him.

"Papa." Donald gets up and runs to his father, he drops next to him and pulls him into his lap. I watch as Richard takes his last few breaths, whispers something to Donald and dies. I holster

PLAYETTE

my gun and smile while Donald cries.

This is part of who I am. I didn't come here to kill him though, I knew the possibility was there, and I don't care anyway. Taking a life doesn't affect me as much as it would someone else, I was molded to know and understand who and when to take one. It's as easy to me now as breathing.

That probably isn't a good thing.

Unless you're me and forced to be this way.

"Donald, I have a business opportunity for you." He looks up, his face is red and blotchy.

"I don't want anything from you bastards," he screams.

"Think carefully, Donald. I gave your father fair warning. Gave him time. He deceived me. You know who we are. Think about this carefully." I walk to him, squat, so I'm at eye-level with Donald. "You can stay here, run this business, and I will take eighty percent of all earnings." I stand, walking out, not waiting for an answer.

My men follow me out to the waiting car. Gabe climbs in after me. Carter takes the passenger seat while Ace drives. My other men follow closely behind.

"Any news on the autopsies?" I ask.

"He's working late tomorrow to do it for us."

"Good." I look out the window. "Tell me, is there anything else?"

"Isadora took Gunner his money tonight." Carter says.

That surprises me. I turn to Carter. "Who told you?"

He smirks. "I've been tracking Benny's car. Benny was at the club and Isadora drove it."

"Why are we tracking Benny?" I ask.

I don't run the club, having no fingers in that pie. This is all on Carter.

"I have trust issues," Gabe mumbles making Carter smile.

"We know," we all reply in unison.

Gabe doesn't like anyone, and trusts no one. It's hard for him to fully trust us at times, but he has to, or at the very least, me. And he does fine in that area. He obeys, and is loyal to a fault.

"Are you going to see why she went?" Gabe asks after we're all silent.

"No."

He looks at me.

"Okay." And I know what he's thinking. Gabe isn't one to question, he simply follows. But I know him well. He's wondering what's so special about her.

The only problem is, I want to know the same damn thing.

I don't want to kill her.

Yet.

And that's a first for me.

CHAPTER 12
Isadora

"HE MENTIONED YOU as well. How could he know?" I ask my uncle as I pace at the front of the car he's currently working on. He slides out, I stop, he shakes his head, and slides back under.

"You know what you have to do."

"No. He isn't my target. I'm not out to kill everyone, uncle. I'm not an out and out fucking murderer."

He laughs from under the car and it echoes. "You are, though. When will you realize that? You're doing what you're best at, seduction and vengeance, on those deserving bastards."

"No. I will *not* do it. He hasn't said anything yet, and maybe he won't."

"I thought I'd taught you better than this?" He slides out and stares at me, he has similar green eyes as me which are the same as my mother's. It's hard sometimes looking at him and seeing my mother staring back at me. I love my uncle, even if his thirst for vengeance is stronger than mine, but I am the one who has to carry out the plan that he implanted into me at a young age.

"I don't trust men." It's a blanket statement, but it has so much truth behind it. "But as I said, I will not go around murdering those that I haven't dreamed about ending, since my mother and father's lives were cut tragically short by those lowlifes."

"That's a shame. I mean, for all your hard work to go to waste."

I smile at him. "I'm starting to think you aren't the best influence that I thought you were, uncle." I turn walking out.

He yells as I leave, "I wouldn't trust them, Isadora. No matter what… a snake is still a snake."

"You did it, didn't you?" I stop as my hand reaches for my door. Turning around I see Sharon standing there.

"Did what, Sharon?"

PLAYETTE

She looks around, her eyes skimming everywhere. "You killed that man, didn't you?"

Reaching for her hand, I pull her inside. "Be careful what you say in public, Sharon." Shutting the door behind her, she looks at me, her eyes assessing me.

"You didn't flinch when that man was found dead, you handled it better than anyone there including the men. I asked around, you were upstairs the night before," she finishes.

"Are you done?" I ask.

Sharon's hands go over her chest and she puffs it up. "I am," and she nods.

"Good," I reply, moving to sit near her. "I would never kill anyone, Sharon. Are you crazy?" I finally respond to her questions.

"I saw the way you reacted... it all adds up. The way you started at work, and the minute you saw those men. I don't know what you're up to, but I know it's something." She finishes off by crossing her arms over her chest.

"Sharon, we're friends, right?" She shakes her head. "Okay, so acquaintances then. And acquaintances don't run their mouths about unnecessary shit. Now, do they?"

She bites her lip, her eyes go down before they come back up to land on me. "Are you threatening me, Issy?"

"Sharon, oh Sharon... now if I was doing that

I wouldn't invite you into my home and offer you a drink." I reach for my mini-fridge and grab a can of Pepsi. "Drink, Sharon?"

She looks at it, back to me then shakes her head.

"No..." she pauses. "You—" Before she can finish, a knock comes at the door.

She swings her head around and I stand to see who's there. Opening the door, Jasper stands there. His eyes fall on my body, raking me over, before he pauses and looks behind me. "You have company?"

I nod, stepping back so he can see Sharon, who's glued to her spot.

"It's probably best you leave," he says to her.

Sharon looks to me quickly before she glances back to Jasper, but I'm not about to make her stay. She should leave, this shit is not something anyone should be messed up in.

"Sharon, this is Jasper." I smile as I say it.

She's heard of him, I know she has from the first time she went to the mansion.

"You're—"

"Leave," he says again.

I step back giving her room to exit. She makes a point of brushing past me and pauses at the door. Jasper steps in, blocks my view, then closes the door in her face. "You had company," he says, stating the damn obvious.

PLAYETTE

"Well, Mr. Obvious, you have a keen eye today," I say with an eye roll. Walking back in I sit on my bed, crossing my legs.

"See, that kind of attitude isn't at all acceptable."

"You're in my place, Jasper. If you don't like it, then leave," I state, waiting for him to react or reply.

He stalks toward me, pushes me back on the bed and drops down so he's leaning over me. He's wearing a white collared shirt with dark jeans. His ink is evident on his arms and the scar on his lip begs to be bitten.

"Do you really want me to leave?" he asks while hovering above my lips.

"Do you always get what you want?"

"Always. It's what's made me so ruthless. People don't like saying no to me." He strokes my face. "Especially women."

I smile, he's left me a great opening. "No, Jasper. How does that sound coming from my lips?"

He shakes his head. "Like you have a heavy desire to be spanked."

I push on his chest, and he lifts up, so I turn until I'm on all fours and bend over in my jeans for him. Looking back so I can see him I say, "Do you want to spank me, Jasper? Tell me I'm a bad, bad girl?"

He stands fully, and in one swift movement he takes off his shirt and drops it to the floor, then he pulls the belt from his trousers and pulls it tight around his hands.

"No tying me up, Jasper," I tell him.

"No touching my back. Do you understand?" I nod. "If you don't listen, Isadora, I will have to tie you up and you may not like what happens after that," he says kicking one shoe off at a time. He then touches the top of his jeans while staring at me.

"Will you fuck me tonight, Jasper?" I ask uttering the words in the most seductive way I can muster.

"If you're a good girl. Otherwise, I'll simply take you, Isadora." I sit and reach for the hem of my shirt pulling it over my head. I'm not wearing a bra.

"Lay down and turn around," he says.

I do as he says, and he steps forward reaching for my jeans and pulls them off with my underwear in one full-on forceful yank. I lay naked in front of him now, waiting for him to speak or touch me, but he does neither.

"What's wrong, Jasper?" I ask sliding up onto my elbows.

He rubs his jaw, while I look down at his cock. It's hard, large, and throbbing. I want it as much as I want him right in this moment.

PLAYETTE

"I wonder if after this, you'll be out of my system?" he asks in the most confused tone.

"And what happens then? Do you kill me? Or perhaps better, not contact me again?" I ask, wanting to know.

"If you warrant death, yes. But so far, you don't. Or, do you, Isadora?" His hand drops from his jaw as he thinks. As he reaches to touch me between my legs, I'm bare and wet for him. It's easily done when you're highly attracted to someone, and I'm absolutely one hundred percent attracted to Jasper.

"Jasper…" I pause. "What's your surname?" I know what it is, but he doesn't need to know that.

"Moretti."

"Ohhh… that makes sense." I nod.

He leans down and in one quick movement, I wrap my legs around his waist and push up pulling him down, so now I'm the one who's looking down on him. The surprise on his face is every bit worth it.

"What the fuck?" He slaps my thighs. "You're strong."

I take the initiative and kiss his lips. He lets me, no sign of hesitation as his hands glide up my bare thighs, and he takes hold of my hips flipping me so fast I'm now on my back. I laugh into his lips and watch as he pulls back and reaches for something. He tears the condom wrapper with his teeth.

I lean up reaching for it. "Let me," I say in my most seductive tone.

He sits back on the bed next to me, his cock sitting tall, waiting, begging to be touched. With a rip I pull the condom from the packet, and lean forward kissing the top of his cock with my lips then letting my tongue skirt out to touch the tip of it. He moans and it's exciting. I don't even have him in my mouth yet, and the want in his eyes is all for me. Making those noises entices me to take him wholly into my mouth, while I still hold the condom in my fingers. His hips thrust upward and his cock goes even deeper, almost into my throat where I'm on the verge of choking, but I somehow resist the urge. Instead, I reach for his balls, rolling them in my fingers as I fuck him with my mouth.

If you've never had the pleasure of making a man go crazy for you, touch you, want you, all because you are touching him, you aren't living your best life.

I know life isn't all about sex.

But it is fun.

Right?

No! It's not? *Yeah, said no one, ever!*

"Is-Isadora…" When my name leaves his lips, just a stutter of my name and the urgency with

PLAYETTE

which he speaks it, I know he needs me in more ways than I'm giving him right now. His fingers thread through my hair, and he pulls me back, takes the condom from my hand and slides it on.

"Jasper. Jasper," I mutter his name a few times.

"You are a naughty girl with an even naughtier mouth." He wipes at my mouth with his thumb.

"I'm a good girl, but I'll be bad for you."

Jasper's thumb slides between my breasts and his cock sits between my legs. I push up, wanting him closer to me.

"Impatient." He tsks at me while shaking his head a few times.

"Needy," I reply arching up again. He pushes down and in a blink he's at my entrance. I can feel him there ready to go, ready to make me his for just one night.

Then what, my mind screams at me. *You get what you want for the night, then what?*

Do I plan to kill him?

Make him drink my potion and force him to fall asleep?

Jasper's phone starts ringing and it does so loudly. He swears a lot, but before he can get up to answer I push up and he slides his tip inside me. He pauses, eyes wide and alert as he looks back to me.

"Needy," he mutters what I've just said.

Ignoring his phone he pushes inside quickly. I reach my hands out to clutch onto the sheets with both hands as he pushes in, again and again. It's like pure fucking heaven, I'm floating on his dick.

Fucking floating.

His mouth makes short work of my nipple, and while he's doing that I do as he says, I don't touch him. Not once do I touch his back. Instead, I keep my hands on the bed, gripping those sheets, while I close my eyes in pure fucking bliss.

Sex is what I'm good at.

I'm better at giving sex, even more so than killing.

I was made to fuck.

And fucking is how I pass my time.

Lifting my chest up a fraction he pushes in harder, his rhythm picking up as his mouth reaches my nipple, and I now know why I wanted him so much. He knows what to do, he knows how to fuck. He's good. Actually, the best, and he's hardly touched me.

He sucks each nipple giving each one attention, all the while he never stops fucking me. His hands touch my body, sliding up and down it until he reaches both breasts and cups my tits then plays with my nipples individually.

It's the hottest thing I've seen. A grown man

PLAYETTE

going crazy over my body, a man as powerful as he is going wild over me.

He doesn't stop, even when I feel my own orgasm building. Jasper removes his hands and slides them down to grip firmly on my hips. He holds them as he takes action, and starts to thrust hard, and when I say hard, I mean it.

I grip the sheets as it comes on, my mind going blank, my head going back and becoming lost in pure fucking bliss.

It isn't long until he comes as well.

And when he does, he pulls out, throws the condom in the bin, and lays next to me.

Jasper Moretti fucks me better than any other man has ever fucked me, and I'm starting to like him. A lot. The excitement he just gave me from coming, instantly disappears at that thought. Dread fills me.

His phone starts right back up.

CHAPTER 13
Jasper

I KNEW THERE was a reason I wanted her so bad, I had to have her. Her body was made for mine. She catches her breath as she lies next to me, and not once did she touch me. For that, I am thankful. I've been with plenty of women where I was fucking them and they still touched me after I told them not to.

"That's really annoying." She turns on her stomach and leans up on her elbows as she looks at me. She nods her head to the phone. "Turn it off already."

"I can't."

She chuckles and touches my stomach. Her fingers begin tracing my heritage tattoo.

"You can. You can take some time off and fuck me all night if you want. Doesn't that sound like a better idea than answering that stupid phone?" Isadora's lips purse together, and I want them back around my cock again. Tight. Sucking. Giving me everything. Just like she was before. My cock stirs and she looks at it.

"See, he agrees with me." Isadora stands, naked. Her body taut and fit, her perfectly shaped breasts sit on her chest, and her brown hair sways as she walks over to the phone. Bending, she shows me her ass and the slit of her cunt as she reaches for it. She flicks a button and my phone powers down. I should be mad. But I smile as she stands up and turns to face me. "Now, isn't that better?" she asks, with her hand on her hip. She walks until she reaches my legs, and pushes against them.

"Dance for me," I tell her.

She steps back and throws her hands above her head and starts to swing her hips in a perfectly synchronized dance. Isadora closes her eyes as she does, and I imagine she's dancing to her own beat in her head. When she opens them again, she stops, drops her hands back to her side and smiles at me. "Tell me you like me," she says, stepping back between my legs.

I'm sitting up, assessing her. "I like you, Isadora. Isn't that obvious considering where I am?" I tell her the truth.

PLAYETTE

"Will you tell me about *her?*" she asks. Leaning down she places her hands carefully on my chest. She then climbs up, straddles me, and smiles as she does so, positioning herself just above my hard cock.

"Who?" I ask reaching for her hips.

She goes down, touches just barely then uses those powerful legs and lifts back up. "Your mother, you mentioned her once. I'd like to know more."

My answer is a simple, "No," I reply, not mincing my words.

"Okay." She pauses, ready to move, and before she can get off me I pull her back down, her mouth opens in a wide O shape as she sits on my dick.

The way her body moves over mine is a sight I will keep in my mind, even when she's testing my every last nerve.

"You..." she breathes but it's breathless, "... cheated," she finishes.

I smile up at her. She hypnotized me and I like it. I like the way she makes me feel lost. And at the same time sane.

My life's nothing but rules and death. It's what I was brought up on. It's like a menu for my life and it's how I know I will die.

It's how my child will rule and die as well.

It's the circle of life in my family.

There's no way out.

There never will be.

I've come to live and learn this. Also accept it as I'm the last breathing Moretti. The rest of my family have been killed off or have died of old age.

And I have to carry on the tradition.

This was my father's last dying wish.

And I hated that fucker, with everything I am.

He ended up being the fucking shittiest father a son could be given.

But he was my father, none the less.

Even up until the day I killed him.

"Jasper..." she stops from touching my chest and concern flashes in her green eyes, "... did I lose you for a second? Are you okay?"

I lift my hand and slap her on the ass. "Move, Isadora."

She does as she's told. She leans in and with the touch of her lips my father's memories are gone and in their place is all her.

What a good way to replace that sadistic prick.

She throws back her head and a smirk touches her lips as her mouth opens in pleasure.

"Jasper." My name on her lips pushes me on, but she stops rocking on my cock, so I take control pushing her forward and back making her orgasm last even longer. Isadora collapses onto my chest, her hair falls over my face as she

PLAYETTE

catches her breath. "I would like to do that again. After my vagina heals, that is."

I touch her hair, it's soft and beautiful. It sprawls out all over my shoulder as she lays there. Stroking my fingers through it, she starts to drift off, then just before she does she bounces up. "Bathroom," she says running.

I wait for her to return and can tell she's washed her face. She walks back over and lays next to me, her head falling back on my chest as I moved to the head of the bed when she was gone.

"This is nice. Do you do nice?"

"No," I reply truthfully.

"You should, sometimes it's good to take a break from a hectic lifestyle." Her green eyes look at me as she waits for me to speak.

"I killed my father, too. Did I tell you that?"

Those beautiful green eyes that were looking sleepy are now wide. Telling her should be a risk, let's be honest though, I could kill her before she speaks of it. Which I won't.

She shakes her head.

"It was his time to give up what I'd worked for and he didn't want to."

Her soft hands stroke my chest. "Did you like your father? Not love him. But maybe like him?" she asks. No one has ever asked me that before. What a strange question.

Did I like him? Before everything I would have answered yes, before he became a ruthless leader who killed everyone in sight that is.

I answer her truthfully. "No. I appreciated who he was as a leader, but not so much as a man. His choices were harsh, brutal, and he didn't see things from a business perspective. He merely saw things the way he wanted them to be. I quickly changed and fixed that. Now I do nothing for personal gain, it's all from a business perspective. For example…" I sit up and face her. "You. I'm fucking you right now because when I do it makes me a better man. I think clearly, and when I don't have you, or sex in general, I become agitated and don't get things right."

"Is that the only reason you're fucking me?" she asks.

"No," I answer.

She smiles.

"I'm fucking you because I want to know what you're hiding. You interest me, and because your pussy tastes like my sweetest treat."

"Talk about making a girl swoon," she jokes, while fanning her face.

"You should get some sleep," I say to her.

"Are you going to stay?" She lays her head back on my chest.

My fingers run through her hair, feeling the silky smoothness. "For a little while."

PLAYETTE

It doesn't take long and she's asleep, and when she does drift off, I'm right behind her closing my eyes.

That never happens.

I sleep alone.

I don't trust anyone.

Least of all women.

And least of all *her*.

CHAPTER 14
Isadora

WHEN I WAKE he's still here, his hands are on my side, as I stayed glued to him during the night. Pulling away, I slide out of bed and notice his phone on the floor. Picking it up, a voice startles me. "I'll take that." I turn to Jasper and notice he's seated in bed, still with no clothes on and looking perfect with his chocolate hair ruffled from all our sex.

Passing it to him, he flicks it on, and when he does it automatically starts ringing. Immediately he answers and puts it on speaker as he stands to pull up his jeans.

"Boss, we know what it was."

I freeze.

Jasper doesn't look at me as he reaches for his shirt, sliding it over his head.

I find my dress lying on the floor and slide that on to cover my naked body.

"And?"

"It's a flower, boss."

Jasper's face scrunches up. "A flower?" he asks, confused.

"Yes, it's a flower. It was in their bloodstreams, both of them."

"How?"

"Doc says, crushed up and digested, more than likely."

I look away as Jasper looks over at me.

"You are sure?" Jasper asks.

"Yep. What kind of flower?"

"Hemlock. It's most harmful ingredient is coniine, which affects the motor nerves and causes paralysis. It's one of the most dangerous plants on the planet. It can take up to three hours for the subject to die." He finishes speaking and how he knows that I have no idea. My heart beats out of my chest and my hands are sweating. I look to my bag, the same bag which holds that plant crushed up and ready to slip into any drink at any time I see fit, it also holds things I need as well if I was to run. Cash, ID, anything I need for my backup plan. Let's face it I would be stupid to not have one.

PLAYETTE

He will kill me. I have no doubt about that fact. Sooner or later, he will.

"Isadora…" Jasper touches my shoulder, making me jump on the spot. "Do you not want me to touch you now?"

I shake my head while faking a smile. "Of course, just daydreaming," I lie.

He leans in and kisses my lips.

I hear a car pull up out the front.

Shit! That was fast.

"I have to go, I want to see you again," he says.

"Okay." It's all I can manage to get out, I'm afraid if I say anything else my words might not make any sense.

He lets me go and walks to the door, I hear him pause, and my heart rate picks back up. "Isadora…"

Turning to look at him, his eyes assess me.

"You'll be here when I get back, right?"

I nod. It's all I can do.

He walks out, shutting the door behind him with a click.

Quickly, I run over, lock it and slide down with my back against the door. Reaching for my phone, I sit up straight and dial my uncle, who picks up on the first ring. "They know."

"Leave, now."

I manage to get my limbs working by climbing

to my feet. Reaching for my bag, it doesn't take me long to pack a few things and grab my purse. Changing into something casual, I pull on a hoodie as well as a beanie which covers my curls.

"ETA?" my uncle asks.

"Ten minutes," I reply, clicking off the cell.

Grabbing my car keys, I fling open the front door but when I do someone pushes me back inside by my chest. Looking up, I notice Gabe standing there with a dirty big smirk on his lips. "I had concerns about you, seems you just confirmed them."

Pushing his hand away I say, "No."

He forces his way inside, shutting the door behind him. In his hand he holds a pistol, his eyes move to the bag in my hand. "Going somewhere?"

"Yes, to visit family," I tell him the truth.

"Tell me, Isadora… who are you, really?" He sits on my bed, and my eyes dart to the door to see if I can make it out before he can react, but all I hear is, "I dare you to try. I haven't shot one of these in a long time. But my aim's always been spot on."

I freeze on the spot as he raises the gun to my eye-level.

"Jasper had to go about his business, but he said you were off. So, here I am," Gabe states looking around. "I like what you've done with

PLAYETTE

the place." He laughs then continues, "Nothing."

"Thanks."

"Planning on a quick exit, hey?"

"Something like that," I tell him a half-truth.

"I need to go to the bathroom," I state.

Gabe stands and walks to the door, looks around checking it out, then steps back out and sits on the bed. He waves his gun at me and says, "Go ahead."

So, I do. Dropping my overnight bag and taking my purse with me, I shut the door behind me. Quickly I grab the baggie of crushed flower, and flush it leaving no trace that I've ever had it.

It's a perfect weapon, potent and deadly. If they hadn't had so many connections, I could have killed so many more. Damn it!

"Girl, hurry up."

I cringe at his words.

Opening the door, Gabe waves the gun around and points to the table. "Sit."

I shake my head. I've been trained for all of this. I have the skills if I need them, I've just never had to use them in a life or death situation before.

"You don't want to sit?" Gabe stands and walks over to me. He's taller than me by a mile. He breathes slowly, deeply, and I feel it on my skin. And those eyes are so alert, vigilant, cautious, they tell me exactly what he's thinking.

"Do you know how they died?" I ask.

"Yes. *You* somehow gave them Hemlock. Well, so I've been told."

"I did."

Gabe looks at me, surprised, like he can't believe I've just admitted it to him.

"Where is it?"

My eyes absently look toward the bathroom, and his eyes follow my movement before they come back to me. "Smart girl. You aren't just a stripper or hooker are you?"

I shake my head.

"Who are you?"

I wave my hand around. "You don't know me, Gabe, but I know you and what you people do. How you take lives that aren't yours to take."

Gabe chuckles at my words. "Are you an *Avenger?* Come to stop us from killing the good?" He steps back from me.

"No Gabe, I've come to kill you. So, no more Moretti Mafia live."

His eyes go wide in surprise but also glimmer with humor. "Girl… that will never happen. We own this town. You can't honestly think you could kill us all. Granted you did a great job with the first two, but honestly, they aren't a great loss, but you did it none the less."

"And you, Gabe, sadly… you are next."

He raises an eyebrow in surprise. "You think you can take me?"

PLAYETTE

I cross my hands over my chest. "Yes," I state categorically.

Gabe leans in close, so close I can feel his breath in my ear. "I would like to see you try, girl."

"Easy." I smile as he pulls back and then kick his shin, hard. He stumbles back and I take the gun from his hand knocking it to the floor, my knee comes up quickly as I reach for his shoulders, and knee him as hard and fast as I can in the balls. He drops.

When he's on the floor, I reach for the gun that he had pointed at me, then raise it until it touches the base of his skull.

He freezes, his movements stop but his hands stay on his balls because he cannot straighten due to the pain. "You wouldn't," Gabe says through gritted teeth.

"I would." I take the safety off and watch as the muscles in his neck tense.

"He'll chase you down, for the rest of his life for betraying him."

I lean down to whisper in his ear, "I hope he does," I say with a smile.

"Why?"

My finger's pressing on the trigger ever so slightly, after I clicked off the safety. "You all killed my family. So, it's simple, I want to take yours."

He gasps and in one moment the gun fires, even with a silencer on it, it's not completely quiet, and the sound that it does make rings through my ears.

Quickly reaching for my stuff, I run to the door and without looking up I slam into another hard body.

"Woah there, pink. Where's the damn fire?"

Oh fuck! It's Ace.

He's going to be harder to kill.

The door clicks behind me and I shove my bag up on my shoulder.

"No fire. Just have to take these clothes into work for the girls." The lie rolls off of my tongue so easily, so smoothly, even I believe myself.

"Okay, pink. But slow down a bit. Let me walk you."

I shake my head. "No," I yell and he squishes his eyebrows together in a frown. "Sorry, I've been stressing about shifts I need to pick up. I have to get in their good books again, since all the time I've been taking off."

Ace steps up to me, touches my shoulder. "You aren't meant to lose money, pink. I'll fix it. You're not meant to be working."

I pat his hand on my shoulder. "Thank you, Ace. I have to go, though. I need to find my own way, make ends meet. Maybe next time we can hang out?"

PLAYETTE

Ace removes his hand and slides it into his pockets. "We can't. Jasper has laid claim to you. I shouldn't even be here right now, but I needed to speak to Gabe." He looks around. "Do you know where he is?"

I shrug as an answer, it's all I can do.

"Okay, he probably went and got something to eat."

I offer him a small smile before I start taking steps to the club which is within walking distance. Passing my car, I cringe knowing I can't get into it straight away because Ace is not far behind me. Walking quickly to the club, I push on the door and I'm glad when it opens and Benny's at the entrance when I arrive. He looks up, shakes his head, and goes back to what he was doing. "What are you doing here, and dressed like that?"

I check the small glass panel through the door and see Ace walking to his car. Without answering Benny's question I state, "I need your car keys, Benny. I have to go. Now." My car is not an option right now.

"Fuck no! Are you crazy?"

I look out the small window in the door once again and notice Ace is walking back to my door with his phone to his ear.

"Benny, please? I wouldn't ask if it wasn't an emergency." He sighs loudly then throws his keys at me. "Thank you. And Benny?" He stops to look at me. "I'm sorry." His eyebrows draw together and he looks at me as if I'm going to say more, but I don't.

Quickly, I slip out the back entrance and to Benny's car.

CHAPTER 15
Jasper

"Boss, the door's locked," Ace says into the phone.

"Where is she?" I ask him as I'm driving back from the mansion to get her.

"She went into the club. Said she isn't getting paid enough because of lost shifts, so she was picking up extra."

"She's fucking lying."

"What? What do you mean?"

"Where exactly did she go, Ace? Find her. Now."

"She hasn't left the club, Jasper. What's the matter?"

"Kick that door in. Now," I tell him.

"Fuck, okay. Hold on."

I wait for him. I hear the sounds of boot meeting wood and then the door swinging open on its hinges to meet the wall with a loud thud.

"Fuck." He doesn't have the phone to his ear, but I can still hear him. "Gabe! Oh fuck! Shit. Fuck." I hear rustling and Ace swearing but that's all.

"Faster," I tell the driver.

"I am, boss."

"Ace," I yell into the phone waiting for him to respond.

"Boss, you aren't going to like this."

"Tell me," I urge.

"Gabe's dead. Bullet to the head."

"Where is she?" I seethe.

"You don't think?" Ace asks.

"It makes perfect sense. Now, find her."

"Got it, boss." He doesn't hang up. Instead, he awaits further instructions from me.

"Don't touch her, only to contain her until I get there."

"Right." And then he hangs up.

It takes five more minutes until we arrive at her place, and when we do, Ace is standing out the front with his leg kicked back on the wall as he scrolls through his phone.

PLAYETTE

He stands up straight when I step over to him, looks behind him to the door that's shut and shakes his head.

"Where is she?" I ask, checking around.

"She left."

"How?"

"She took Benny's car."

I smile. Good! Because that car has a tracker on it.

"You've tracked her already, I hope?"

Ace shows me the screen, the blip shows she's paused at a warehouse not that far from here. "Seems she's stopped. Should we pay her a visit?"

"Yes, but first…" Opening the door, I see Gabe lying with a pool of blood around his head. "She did this?"

Ace nods. "Checked the security camera footage myself… camera's just over there." He points to a shitty looking convenience store. "Seems only Isadora and Gabe were here at the time. It had to be her."

"Fuck."

"Yep, who would have thought?" Ace states out loud, but you can tell he actually meant to keep it to himself.

"You need to run a background check, make it as deep as you can. She's been hiding something. I want to know what it is, and I want to know

now."

"You got it, boss."

I fell asleep next to her and didn't think she was capable of this. I liked her, I liked her a lot, and that is very unlike me. Maybe it's the crazy I attract because I'm fucking crazy. I step away as Ace calls the cleaners and I call her.

I'm surprised when she answers.

"Jasper." Her voice sounds off.

"Isadora," I breathe into the phone. "You've been a bad girl, it seems."

"So, it seems," she says right back at me.

"You know you can't hide from me, right?"

"Oh, but I'm not hiding. I'm currently staring at Carter. Maybe you should say goodbye to him, while you still can."

"Isadora…"

"It makes me crave you when you say my name like that."

"Where are you?"

"You don't know where your men are? Carter was easy to find, and you idiots helped my cause."

"And what cause is that?" I slide in the car as the cleaners arrive to get rid of Gabe's body and remove any trace of the murder taking place. I don't want this to come back on us.

"You still haven't worked it out yet, Jasper? I heard you're smart. What's happening?" I run

PLAYETTE

my hand through my hair. "Are you planning all the ways you want to fuck the truth from me, Jasper? Or, all the ways you can kill me?" she asks. I hear the soft sound of music coming through the speaker of the phone.

"Bit of both," I tell her honestly.

"I bet you're wishing you kept me tied to the bed right now," she says as the music becomes louder.

"I do."

"Carter, say hey to Jasper."

"Hey, boss." I hear Carter's voice and turn to Ace, while covering the speaker of the phone. "Call Carter, right now."

"Jasper, do you think what you do is okay?" she asks quietly. "That taking lives which aren't yours to take… that it's okay?"

"Yes, I can do what I want, when I want."

"So, maybe I can, too. Have you thought of that?"

"Boss, hurry up," Carter yells out in the background.

"I wonder if he knows about Hemlock," she whispers.

"Don't you dare," I seethe.

"Carter, tell Jasper what drink you just had?"

"Just a beer, boss," he yells.

"Put him on the phone."

She laughs. Shit! I want to spank her, fuck her, kill her and I want to do it all at the same time.

"He's funny, Carter. Did you know your boss is funny?"

"There's no going back from this, Isadora," I warn.

"Oh, I know, Jasper. And to think I like you."

"You do? And I like you, Isadora. That's why it's going to kill me to have to kill you."

She laughs maniacally into the phone. "You can try, Jasper. But you will come to find I am hard to kill." She hangs up on me and I look to Ace.

"No answer, boss."

"Fuck."

Seems I say that a lot when it involves Isadora—a lot more than I care to admit.

She's going to be hard to kill, but she's signed her own death warrant. And killing my men, yeah, that's not going to be tolerated, for any reason.

CHAPTER 16
Isadora

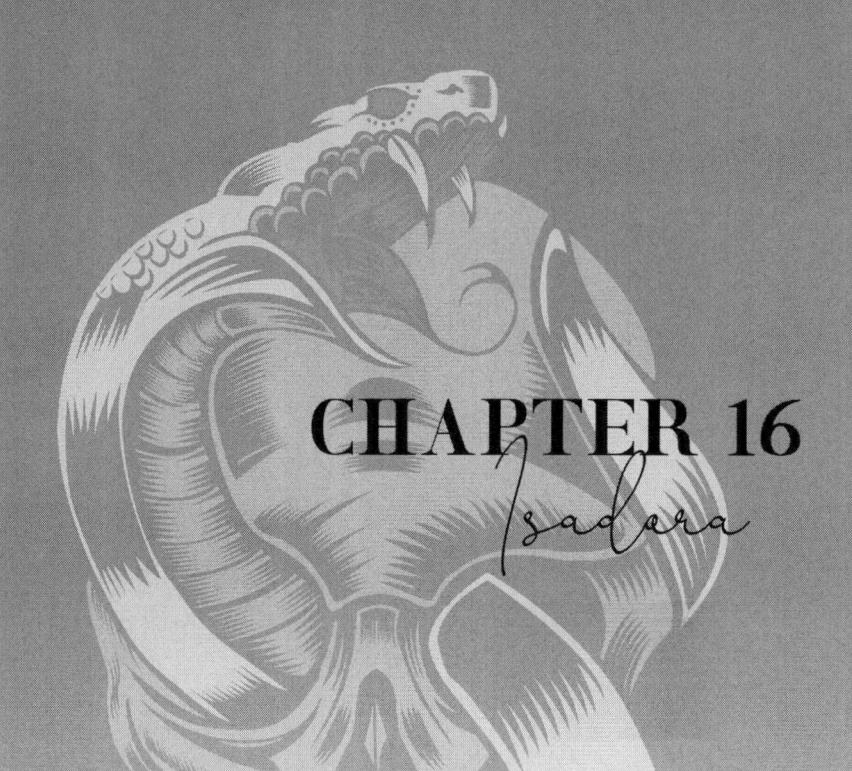

"HE LIKES YOU, you know," Carter says, while chugging down his drink. I have to look away as I like him too, and when I do my eyes avert to my phone which is ringing.

And one guess who it might be? Yes, Jasper.

"Does he?"

"Oh, yes, and he doesn't like anyone. Not even me. And I'm his second in command." He chuckles taking another swallow. "He didn't want to let Mack in the family…" he talks about the dude I killed first, "… but I ended up talking Jasper into it."

Mack needed to die, so I don't feel one bit of

guilt over the part I took in taking his life. Mack was fucked-up in more ways than one anyway.

"Mack was your brother?"

Carter nods. "Yep, he was fucked-up. Always had been. But we gave him purpose, and that helped him a little, even if Jasper hated him."

"Jasper hated Mack?" I ask.

"Yep. But we were born into this, the same way Jasper was. We're family after all, and despite what happened we love him, and the respect we hold for him is above the rest. It's part of the reason we follow him with no questions asked. Ever."

"What did he do?"

"You heard of his father?" he asks, taking another sip of his beer.

"He told me some things." I tell him the truth.

Carter looks me over. I'm still wearing jeans and a jacket, though I did lose the beanie. "He told you about him?"

"That he killed him."

Carter's mouth opens, obviously not quite believing that Jasper confided in me. "He did. But he doesn't talk about it."

"Why not?"

"He idolized him. He was his father. At the beginning, his father protected him from his mother."

"But he killed her, too," I say remembering his

PLAYETTE

conversation.

"Fuck! How are you here with me, if he likes you this much?" he asks.

I shrug, not answering that question.

"Well, I should stop drinking. My mouth tends to shoot off and I tell too much when I do."

I wave the bartender over and order four shots. "Jasper's coming here. So, let's have some fun before the boss arrives. Agreed?"

Carter nods his head.

It takes six more shots before he starts speaking again.

"Did you know his mother?" I'm a little drunk myself, probably not the best idea because I won't be on my game, but I need to get him talking and if I have to go shot for shot then I will do it.

"Yeah, she was a real piece of work," Carter spits. "That bitch tortured him. You've seen his back, right?" I nod. "Well, that little piece of artwork was all her."

"Shit."

Carter nods. "Damn right, shit! That bitch was crazy." He chuckles.

"And his dad protected him?" I ask, confused as to why anyone would hurt someone they love so much.

"Until he was thirteen." He shudders. "Then his father, well... he stopped caring. Left his mother and Jasper. He would only come around Jasper when he had people to kill, so he used him for that... you know, to carry out the kills."

"When was his first kill?"

"Fourteen." Carter slaps the bar with his hand and the bartender walks over and pours us both another shot. I don't drink it, so Carter drinks mine as well. "Yep, that's some fucked-up shit. Right? His father lost his shit, too. The taste of power and money became so much, and so completely ingrained in him, that when Jasper turned eighteen he put a bullet through his father's skull in the mansion. It's why he built that place out back to live in. He hates that fucking mansion and his father's room."

"I have to go." I stand, but I start swaying.

Shit! I knew drinking was a bad idea.

"Oh look, Jasper's here."

I freeze as I slide Carter's phone back into his pocket and walk out the back. Just before I reach the door a hand touches my hip and pulls me back.

"Darling, you aren't running from me, are you?" I spin in his grasp and reach up to kiss his lips, and for some reason he lets me. He even kisses me back. It's soft and hard all rolled into one.

"Jasper," I say his name and I bet he can taste all my bad choices.

PLAYETTE

"Isadora..." he breathes, pulling away from my lips, "... you've been a bad, bad girl. Haven't you?" He looks down and realizes why I kissed him, I have a knife in my hand directed at his crotch. "Isadora, you may get to leave. But I *will* find you."

"I'm counting on it, Jasper." Leaning in again, I kiss his lips then pull away lifting the knife from his cock and smiling.

I slip out the back door and run as fast as I can. It takes me close to an hour to get back to my uncle—my feet are hurting and my head's thumping in pain.

"You're drunk." My uncle shakes his head as I wobble on not so very straight legs. Pretty sure I may have ran into a few bushes along the way too.

"No."

"Let me guess, you didn't kill the other one?"

"No."

My uncle huffs loudly, walking past me and shutting the door behind me. "You need to get rid of this car, for all you know they've already tracked it."

"Yeah, I will." I crawl onto a mattress on the floor in his office and crash.

"Fuck, you're so beautiful."

I jump and sit bolt upright on the mattress. Jasper is standing over me and looking directly at me. I slide my hand under the pillow and come into contact with my knife.

"Do you really think that's a good idea?" He nods to the pillow, indicating the knife I now have firmly gripped in my hand.

"Where is he?"

"Do you mean that man who tried to stop me from coming in?" He looks behind him and pulls out the office chair. He takes a seat and rests his gun which is firmly grasped in his hand on his lap.

How is it possible for him to look this good? It's totally unfair actually, especially when I know I look like shit.

"Yes." Fucking hell, he better not have hurt my uncle, he's the only family I have left in this world considering this bastard and his family took mine away from me.

Jasper taps the gun on his knee, then he bites his lip, the one with the scar, and I remember how good he tasted last night. Before he says another word the door opens and Carter steps in, looking as bad as I feel, he cringes when he sees me.

"Boss." I can now hear the grunting of my uncle as the door is wide open. "This bastard is strong and he's not talking." Carter shuts the door, leaving us to ourselves.

PLAYETTE

"You played me well. Too damn well. I knew there was something up with you, I just couldn't put my finger on it. Who would have thought a girl who works at a strip club could be on a big vendetta. You truly are remarkable. We could've been a great team…" he chuckles, "… we could've ruled the fucking world." Jasper stands and my heart jumps a beat.

"It would never have worked, Jasper. You kill for the fun of it. What normal person does that?"

He cracks his neck from side to side, closing his eyes as he rolls his shoulders. "I'm meant to kill you. I should kill you on the spot, right here, right now. I've done it before. Carter told you about my father, he tells me everything, but what he didn't tell you was how I killed my mother." He drops to a squatting position so we're at eye-level. "Would you like to know?" I shake my head in answer but he continues anyway with, "Too bad."

He stands, and begins pacing the room. Back and forth. He doesn't pay me much attention, he's too lost in his own head. I know if I move he'll kill me. It's what men like him are made to do. It's what he was born to do. He is his father's son after all.

"She was beautiful, did you know that? So fucking beautiful. It was hard to stay angry at her when she smiled, it made me think I was the most important person in the room." His eyes take on that faraway look as if he's seeing her standing here, right now, in this room with us. "She reminds me of you, actually. Your beauty could rival hers. And trust me when I say, not many could. It's how she got my father, the most powerful man in the world, to fall in love and impregnate her so she could trap him." He pauses. "You see, I was never what she wanted. I was simply the means to hold Father. She wanted power. She wanted money. Both of which my father had. What she didn't expect was for him to love me in ways she couldn't. And in the end he loved me more than her. Even as I put the gun to his head, he told me that."

"I'm sorry," I say when he pauses for a long time, the silence is deafening.

"Don't be. He deserved to die. It was his time. He'd out-lived, and out-killed more than he deserved."

A loud bang comes on the door. Jasper turns to pull it open but only halfway. He looks back to me and smiles. "Take him to my house." Then he shuts the door again.

Turning around to face me, he slides his gun into the back of his pants. "I'm not going to lie, I loved my father. Even with all the bad things he did, I still loved him, as much as you're trained to love someone, and in his own way I know he loved me, too. Love… it's a fickle bitch, isn't it? We kill those we love. I've killed two people I

PLAYETTE

loved and I probably could have loved you, too, Isadora. Yet, now, it's my turn to kill you. It seems like that's what life wants from me... to kill those I love."

His words shock me, they can't be true.

He doesn't care for me, does he?

I thought I was just another plaything to warm his bed.

It seems I'm mistaken.

Standing, I walk over, careful to not touch him, and when I'm in front of him I attempt to stand as tall as I can muster. "Why must you be the devil, it's very unfair."

Jasper touches a stray piece of my hair and pushes it behind my ear. "She smiled at me, did I tell you that? As I put the gun to her head, she smiled her beautiful smile. It was dazzling. I told her I loved her before I pulled the trigger. She told me she didn't love me. It was bittersweet. Almost poetic. Now tell me, Isadora..." he holds the back of my neck in place as his lips come close and he whispers, "... how yours died."

I say nothing, no words can escape my lips.

He knows.

He knows exactly who I am.

That means he also knows who killed my parents.

I start shaking my head back and forth, but he doesn't let me go, keeping me firmly in place.

"Jasper." It's a plea, for what I don't know, but his name leaves my lips nonetheless.

"Do you think you could have loved me?" he asks as his lips brush mine.

I give him the answer he wants to hear. "No." I say it with enough conviction that even I might believe it. He slams his lips onto mine and demands for me to open my mouth. I let him in, and kiss him passionately because I know this will be our last kiss, our last embrace. His hand moves and I feel something sharp at the base of my neck, I pull back as it pricks me, and notice there's a needle in his hand.

"Don't worry," he whispers. "It's not Hemlock, but it will make you pass out."

My head becomes dizzy and before I can fall he catches me and picks me up bridal style. "You might just be my toughest kill yet, Isadora."

I should have run when I had the chance, but I couldn't, and now here I am in the arms of a man who wants to kill me, one who's as complex as my feelings.

And that's the last thing I remember before my eyes become too heavy and close.

CHAPTER 17
Jasper

HER EYELASHES ARE long, she makes soft sounds as she lays on my lap.

"Boss." Ace turns around from the front seat, looks down at her and back to me. "Do you plan to kill her?"

I know he likes her. Let's face it she's easy to like. I run my fingers through her hair as we come to stop at the front of the mansion. I don't use the damn mansion, I can't. My men occupy it, every inch of it, except his room. That was the room where I took *his* life, and now it's a testimonial to everything he was. I haven't been in there since the day he died, but as I walk the stairs with Isadora in my arms I know that's the place she needs to be.

"Boss, are you sure?" There's no point answering him, I've made up my mind and once it's made up it's difficult to shift. That's why I still haven't decided if I plan to take her life, or to keep her locked away so I can see her and do to her anything I like at any time.

"The uncle's making noise," Carter says rounding the corner.

"Let him." I chuckle. "It's going to be fun to watch that bastard squirm."

Isadora starts moving in my arms as Carter opens the door to *that* room. With her in my arms I kick the door shut behind me, so it's just us.

The sheets have been changed, but the room remains the same. It's like he's downstairs and I'm sneaking into his room to do something completely disobedient—like I am a child again. Walking to the bed, I lay her on the thick mattress. She turns over, rolls into a ball and snores softly. Getting up, I take off my shirt and reach for the ties I know are still in the drawer. Taking one hand at a time, I fasten her to the bed, so her arms are spread and her face looks upward. She starts to stir, when I knot the tie around her feet. She's now tied and bound like a starfish.

Walking around the bed, I touch her face by running my finger down the side of her cheek, waiting for her to rouse.

PLAYETTE

She stirs, those beautiful green eyes look up to me. She goes to move but nothing happens. She struggles and pulls on the bindings, but they are too tight for her to be able to loosen. There's no way she's shifting an inch or getting away from me.

"Jasper." She calls my name.

I sit next to her, my fingers playing on her belly then up between her breasts as I pull out the knife she has hidden between them. Her eyes go wide at my finding it, and when I do I cut the shirt and jacket from her body, so her tits are free and all she has on is her jeans.

"I hope you aren't fond of your clothing, Isadora." The knife glides ever so slowly down her bare skin until it reaches her belly button. "Honestly, I thought your name would be fake, I was surprised to learn you gave me your real one."

"I like my name. I'm named after my grandmother."

"I like it, too, Isadora. Now what do I do with you?"

"Guess that's up to you, now, isn't it?"

"What would you do, Isadora?"

She tries to lean up but she can't and it frustrates her so she pulls at her bindings. "I would kill you all," she shouts, then smiles and lays her head back.

"You see... now I know that's a lie. Because you had the chance to kill Carter and you didn't take it. I know you know how to, you're actually quite good at it. Who would have thought to carry out the murders of my men using that method? Was it you, or the uncle? Who's the bright spark in this so-called relationship of yours?"

"Me," she says proudly.

"I thought so." The knife slides to her jeans and I start cutting. Her jeans tear easily with how sharp this small paring knife is and soon she's lying on the bed naked. "It's perfect really to have you like this. In the same place I killed *him*."

She looks around. "Is this?" She tries to arch her back to get off the bed but once again the bindings hold tighter, the knots I used will only tighten the more she struggles. I can see her hands losing their blood supply. "Oh my God... am I on *his* bed?" Her eyes go wide and her top lip lifts a little like it disgusts her.

"Quite poetic isn't it, when you think about it?"

"Jasper, you don't love me. You can't, to put me here."

I shake my head. "Don't I?" I ask while sitting back and gazing over her naked body. "No woman's sent me bat-shit crazy as much as you have. Why is that, I wonder?"

"Because I hold your interest."

PLAYETTE

"I kill those I love, Isadora. So you should hope that it's simply infatuation. But I'm having my doubts. I knew you were special from the first night I met you, and then when I kissed you I knew I'd want more, and that hasn't changed. I still want you, even now as I find out you killed my men and have betrayed me. The single two worst things you can do to me."

"You destroyed me," she yells with tears streaming down her cheeks. "Destroyed me! Now kill me, so we can get this over with."

I lean down and lick the tears which have trickled down her cheeks, she turns away so her lips aren't accessible to me. Gripping her face hard, I turn her back to me, taking each and every one of them, savoring every moment. She's worth savoring.

"I can't. Not yet anyway."

She doesn't look at me. I climb over her body, so I'm sitting on top of her as I drop the knife on the bed while my fingers start to circle the shape of her breast. Then they circle her nipples. They snap to attention in small taut buds, all the while she's looking away not wanting to make eye contact with me.

"You really do fascinate me," I tell her, running my fingers down her belly until I reach her pussy. Touching the outside, running my fingers up her slit, she squirms, so I dip my finger in just a touch and I can feel her warmth.

"I hate you," she mumbles.

"I know," I say back while leaning down, holding her face with my free hand, turning it to look at me, and I kiss her lips as I insert a long finger inside her.

She moans into my mouth, her legs pull against the restraints, but that only helps me to open them even more.

I kick my trousers off as I lift up from her lips and touch my cock. Pumping it a few times, as she watches my every move, even as I slide it between her legs. And as I do they part automatically for me this time. Now they are out as far as they can go considering she's tied, and I slide straight inside of her.

It's pure fucking magic.

She is pure fucking magic.

It's going to be hard to kill her.

Sliding in and out, and claiming her kisses, Isadora doesn't speak or say another word, but she lets me claim her and she enjoys every second of it.

Isadora may hate me, but she craves me as much as I crave her.

"Fuck you," she says as I push in a lot harder.

"I am... fucking you." I push in again then lean down to bite her nipple. Hard. I leave my mark there, and go to the next doing the same. She feels like everything I have ever wanted.

PLAYETTE

She's the place you dream of moving to. She is *my* place.

"I hate you," she cries out in pleasure.

"You said that already, it's getting boring," I remind her as I continue to fuck her.

The door opens and her eyes shift straight to it, but I continue my rhythm as though nothing in this world is worth stopping this heaven for.

She's worth a thousand suns and to kill her will extinguish all light.

CHAPTER 18
Isadora

HE PUSHES IN, and out, not stopping at all, not allowing me any rest or the ability to catch my breath while Ace stands in the doorway. Ace's eyes go from me to Jasper, who's between my legs and there isn't a thing I can do about it. The fucked-up thing is I don't want him to stop because it feels too damn good. And I know this is probably the only pleasure I'll get for a long while or before I'm dead.

"Boss, you're needed."

Jasper turns to look at Ace with a smile on his face as he pauses inside of me.

Damn! I was so close. So close I can't help myself and lift my pelvis to make his cock move inside of me again.

"Are you jealous, Ace?" Jasper moves at an agonizing slow pace.

"Yes, sir," Ace replies. Ace's eyes come back to me, and so do Jasper's.

"Maybe I will let you fuck her."

My eyes go wide.

"Would you like that, Isadora, two cocks in you?"

My mind's screaming at me to say no.

I should say no, right?

"Look at that, Ace. She isn't sure." Jasper pushes in and then back out, then he leans down so our lips are touching. "I don't share, Isadora, you *will* learn that fact."

When I look back to where Ace was standing, he's gone. It's now just Jasper and myself yet again.

"You're fucked-up, you know that?"

"Oh, darling, I know. It's perfect, and you know why? Because you're just as fucked as me. The perfect pair, surely."

I shake my head.

He pushes in harder and faster, his pace picking up. If I had the movement of my legs I'd wrap them around him right now. Instead, I bite my bottom lip as the orgasm hits me and it hits me hard.

He crashes his lips onto mine to stop the moan

PLAYETTE

that wants to leave. However, I can't kiss him back because I feel almost paralyzed, my body being taken over by the intensity of the orgasm.

Jasper is by far the best lover I've ever had. I think he's aware of that fact as well. He gets delight out of my pain, but also from my pleasure.

He's a giver, and I love to take.

When he pulls back, his cock slides out of me. Jasper kneels between my open legs looking down with a smirk so deadly I almost lose my breath when he drops his head between my legs and kisses my clit then punishes it with his tongue. I squirm around on the bed, an orgasm building quickly again from his touch, and just before I head over the precipice he stops. A kiss is all I get before he looks at me with our sex all over his lips.

"This is the perfect place to say our goodbye. Don't you think, Isadora? Fucking you on the bed that I killed my father in? Yep, it's poetic at best." He climbs off the bed and walks over to his jeans, pulls them back on, and I watch as he tucks his cock back in. And when he's fully dressed, he walks to the door and looks back at me. "It's probably time you start praying." Then without another word he shuts the door as he leaves.

I can feel his cum leaking out of me.

Did he do that on purpose? Mark me one last time?

I pull on the restraints hoping that I can somehow slip my hand through, but it's tied tight and all I can feel is pins and needles as I keep on trying. Pulling on my feet, I come to the same conclusion. *I'm fucked.*

A scream echoes through the house and I wonder what they're doing to my uncle or if maybe that was him dying. I really hope not. Despite him never loving me, he's the only family I have left, and I don't want him to die.

My eyes become heavy, but I'm afraid to fall asleep. What will I find if I wake up, and that's a big *if* I wake up. He could kill me in my sleep, and I would be none the wiser, I don't think that's Jasper's way, though. From everything I've learned about him he's not impulsive. He thinks hard about everything he does. Everything I've studied about him is that he's a man of deliberate action. Dangerous. More so than his father. People speak of him as if he's a warrior. He's fearless and they're too afraid to say his name. I should've listened to the whispers back then, but that wouldn't have helped my cause, though. My heart starts pounding and my vision blurs, fear takes root in my core and I wonder how I will ever get out of this situation or if this will be my end.

Turning my head to the side, I check around the room. I'm on a four-poster bed. It's large. The room smells like a storage unit, just like it should

PLAYETTE

do seeing as obviously no one comes in here. Maybe that's the way he likes it. The room's empty and plain.

Right in front of me, where a television should sit is a large picture of a woman with light brown hair, tinges of sun-kissed blonde streaks through it. She's in a short dress, it's white, and in her arms is a small baby. I wonder if this is his mother in the photograph. She's certainly perceived as a caring woman, looking down at her baby with a smile so bright it's dazzling. I can see Jasper in her features, his high cheekbones definitely come from her. Turning my head away from the picture that's full of lies, I see the room is painted in a light blue almost aqua with splashes or flecks of gold through it. It's unlike the rest of the house which is a plain cream. This room, and the size of this room, it was designed for a king and his queen. From the top of the bedposts, which are gold, to the gold flicking on the walls.

To the left is a large open closet with clothes still hanging in there—men's suits.

My eyes become heavy and I can't keep them open for a second longer. Sex usually puts me to sleep, and it's trying to do so right now.

Even with my sore wrists and tied ankles, I manage to close my eyes and dream of a life I once had—braided hair, sunlight kisses, and looks of pure devotion from parents who would do anything for me.

I dream of them.

And what was taken away from me.

"Momma," I scream. She comes running out the shop, her eyes searching frantically. Her hair so long I wish mine would grow like that. I'm fourteen, and my boobs are only just starting to form.

"What's wrong?" She checks around and I look down between my legs, her eyes go wide. "Oh, sweet girl, it's okay."

My head starts to shake back and forth. "It's not. I'm bleeding and I have a date. My first one, ever," I scream.

"It's okay, Isadora. Trust me. It's what happens when you become a woman." Her fingers brush my messy hair back from my face, and she pulls me in for a hug and I smell her, she smells of cakes and pastries. It's what she always smells like. She's one of the best cooks and the prettiest.

"I'm already a woman," I tell her pulling away.

"Of course, you are, my dear." She reaches for my hand and pulls me to the back of the bakery.

My father smiles at me despite looking down and seeing blood all over my white trousers.

"Run upstairs and grab a washcloth, some new clothes and panties and come back down. I have some things I need to teach you." I do as Momma says, running up the stairs and getting everything she asked for. I find my favorite dress, clutching it in my hands, I run back down the stairs.

PLAYETTE

Voices are the first thing I hear. They stop me on the second to last step. I'm frozen in position unable to move.

My mother's voice is high-pitched and it's got a tone to it I'm not really sure of, which stops me from going any further.

"Please. Please, I beg of you, just leave." She's pleading with someone.

My hands clutch the railing as my foot touches the last step.

"That can't happen."

I don't know that voice, it's strong, though. It's not my father's, whose voice follows. "You can't. This is all wrong. You can't do this."

Upon hearing his voice, I step around the corner, and a hand touches my shoulder pulling me back as the first bang goes off. I watch in absolute horror as my mother drops to the floor – a man standing in front of her with a gun in his hand and a smile on his face.

"No." My father screams dropping to the floor, touching her face, which isn't moving.

"Kid, run." I'm pushed as another loud bang sounds.

I don't know what to do.

My legs still have blood on them, there's fresh clothes in my hands and they stay there as I start to move.

My eyes spring open and I can't help the tears

that leave them as they fall freely down my cheeks remembering that day, the worst of my life. My parents loved each other more than I could ever dream of. They loved me with a fierceness that I'm afraid I will never experience again.

It breaks my heart.

All over again.

Every time I think of them, my heart shatters a little more.

"Your tears are like music to my soul. I want them all the time." Jasper sits on the floor, against the door with his knees up, as he watches me.

"Why am I waking up?" I ask, not even bothering to make an excuse for the fact that I'm crying.

"Because I choose it."

"Just do it already. What pleasure do you get from this?" I ask, waiting for him to tell me why.

He pushes up from his seated position, and turns to walk out the door. "I'm still trying to work myself up to it, Isadora. Killing you is proving to be harder than I thought, and it won't be one of my finer moments," he says as he walks out. His words hurt, more than they should. I should have been easy to kill, he should have been easy to kill. But our emotions have come into play, and no matter how much I try to deny all of them, they are there and evident. Now, if I

PLAYETTE

could only slow my pounding heart when he enters a room, or dry my hands, sweaty with the need to touch him, this could be so much easier.

CHAPTER 19
Jasper

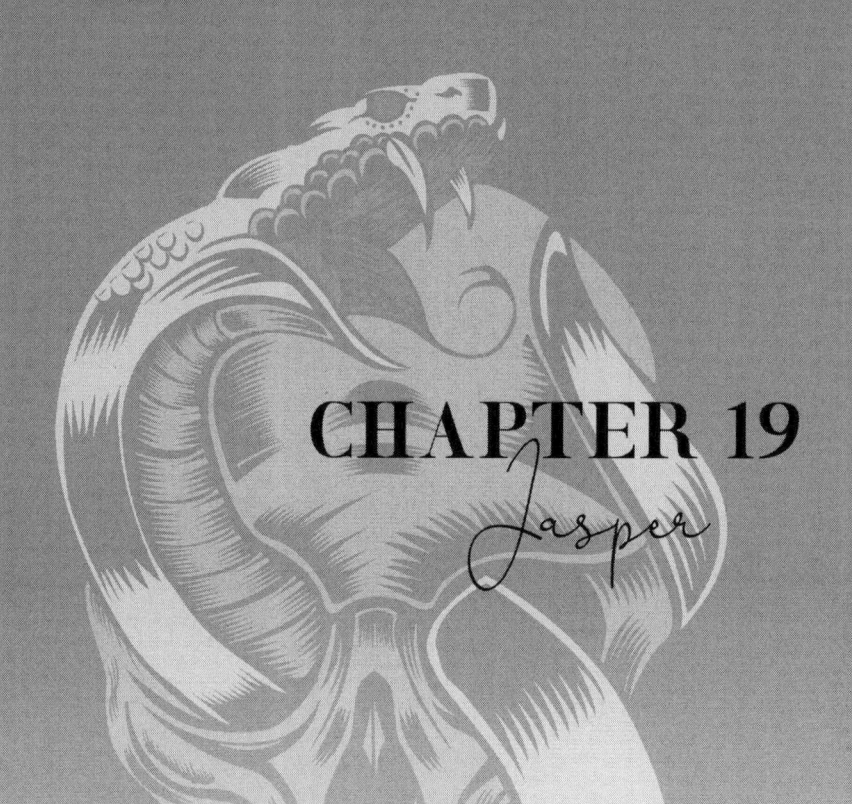

*H*AVE YOU SEEN *an angel sleep?* I have, and what a fucking angel she is.

I came into the room with a purpose in mind—to kill her.

It's an easy task. I've killed people as easily as I breathe. It's natural to me. It is, after all, what my father taught me to do. Who he wanted me to be.

I'm exactly what my mother beat into me.

When I walk back into the room she's asleep again. Isadora's tears are dried on her cheeks as I sit down next to her. Running my hand down her bare leg, I start to untie her one leg at a time.

When she's free, I lift and carry her to my father's bathroom, turning the shower on and placing her on the floor. She wakes as I climb in fully clothed and sit behind her, holding her to me. When she starts to move, my arms lock firmly around her body.

"I need to pee," she states.

"Pee then. The shower will wash it away."

Her body relaxes into mine as the water becomes warmer. I push her hair back and kiss her neck until she falls into me.

"I still hate you," she says.

"I know," I reply. "I know."

Tears fall freely now.

Reaching for the shampoo I start to wash her hair as she lays back on my chest and then rinse it out. She stays where she is not moving. Grabbing the loofah, I wash her body, around her tits and down to her pussy until she's all clean and smelling like magnolia blossoms.

"She would tie me up, in her bathroom... and whip the fuck out of me as if I was a damn toy. With a bottle of wine in her hand and a whip in the other. Her father was a master with the whip and taught her how to use it effectively. She was brilliant... in so many ways," I tell her then kiss her neck.

"How can you say that?"

I shrug. "Sometimes you have to look beyond

PLAYETTE

the hurt to see something else. I saw it in her. Always did, even on that fateful day."

"I watched my mother die in front of me. I wasn't meant to, I don't think," she tells me, but I already know her story. However, I'll let her tell me anyway.

"Maybe you weren't meant to," I tell her. "Maybe that's what made you the woman you are today? You needed that strength, and that strength came from witnessing what happened to your family."

Her head starts shaking back and forth. "No, I don't believe you. Watching the people you love be murdered… ah fuck! The hurt does nothing but break your soul and tear your heart into pieces." Isadora pushes up and away from me, she's standing looking down at me while I'm still fully clothed. "You're incapable of love. And that's not your fault, Jasper. That shit's the fault of your mother not showing you how love is meant to be." She takes a deep breath and her tits rise as she does. "My mother showed me what love is. I was given that and more, but it was violently taken from me." She steps out of the shower, as if I've given her permission to do so.

I haven't.

Standing and tearing off my shirt, I pull at my jeans as they fall in the water before I step out coming face to face with her.

"You don't plan on killing me, do you?"

"I'm working up to it," I tell her the truth.

"It's not something you should have to work up to, Jasper." She tries to cover her breasts but it doesn't work. "Is my uncle still alive?"

I cringe. "I wouldn't worry yourself about him."

Her back straightens. "Is he alive or not, Jasper? Just answer the damn question, it's simple enough."

"He's alive… *for now.*"

"You aren't tying me back up again," she tells me as if she has a choice in this matter.

"You seem to forget what you've done, Isadora. Has it slipped your mind that you killed three of my men? One being Carter's brother. Do you know what we do to traitors?"

"Kill them," she says, but I shake my head.

"No, that's too easy. First… I find the one thing they love the most. Then, I make them watch as I destroy that one thing. Tell me, Isadora, who do you love the most?" I can see she wants to say her uncle, it's on the tip of her tongue, but she pauses as the door clicks in the bedroom and I reach for a towel wrapping it around my waist then handing one to her.

"What do you want from me?" she asks as I open the door of the bathroom.

Isadora follows me out, and when she sees

PLAYETTE

who's standing there she stops in her tracks. "Heather," she says, the words are barely a whisper from her lips. "You need to go. Just go. Now."

Heather shakes her head and steps up to me, her soft little hand comes to lay on my arm. "Jasper promised me. He promised me, Issy."

Isadora turns an accusing look my way. "What did you promise her? She's innocent in this." She tries to defend her friend.

"She doesn't care for you, Isadora, all Heather wants is power. She thinks I can give it to her. So, in exchange, she's been getting close to you, making you trust her, all the while she spies on you for me."

Isadora's beautiful green eyes go wide, her hand clutches the towel she's holding to her chest as though she's in pain. "You wouldn't."

Heather's sweet face turns sour. "I didn't lie to you when I told you about me. I just happened to leave out that I'm fine, and that I'm not as hopeless as you think me to be."

"I didn't think you were hopeless," Isadora says, and I can see the pain in her eyes.

It's a pity Heather feels none of that. She would come to me every night and tell me about Isadora. It was easy to get her to do what I wanted. After that first night I saw her standing outside while I was smoking, I wanted to know more about her, and Heather was an easy way in. Heather would come and tell me what she wears, who she served, where she lived, what she had in her home, every damn thing I needed to know. And I knew everything, all thanks to Heather. She's an easy catch, in exchange for, what? Me saying I'd keep her.

I didn't say how, and quite frankly, I don't think she cared. She only cares for what she can run her mouth about, and how much money she can make from running her mouth.

She's simply a climber, and I have no time for people like her. The only reason she's near me right now is to ruffle Isadora's feathers, and it's working extremely well.

"It doesn't matter. You had what I wanted. Didn't you think it was weird that I suddenly started to get to know you, Isadora? I do that to most of the girls, to see who's working at the club for the right reasons or who's a spy. I didn't think you were until that night you didn't want me to come here. You really should work on your poker face, Issy." Heather finishes speaking, her hand slides up and down my bare arm.

That's a no.

A big fucking no.

I remove her hand and step away.

Isadora notices and smiles.

"You should leave, Heather, before I get

PLAYETTE

angry," Isadora says, and I see fire in her eyes.

"You don't scare me, Issy. You're locked in a room with the most ruthless man in this town. It's not you I'm scared of, you idiot."

"It should be," I mutter to Heather making her head swing my way.

"What? You still want this whore?" Isadora straightens her stance at the use of that name from Heather.

"Leave, Heather, and take your lying mouth with you." Isadora steps forward, but Heather shakes her head. "No. Maybe I'll fuck Jasper in front of you. See if you like that?"

I balk at the thought — it will never happen.

Not in this lifetime.

The only hands I want touching me are currently scrunched into fists, her jaw's clenched, nostrils flared, and there's a definite angry look haunting her beautiful face.

"Try it," Isadora says, dropping her head to the side in defiance.

Heather starts to walk over to me and within two seconds Isadora crosses the room and has her hands around Heather's throat, and slams her against the wall. "I fucking liked you, Heather. Pity you had to ruin it." Isadora serves a hard hit to Heather's abdominal area and then drops her hand from her throat and she crashes to the floor then looks up at me.

"Are you going to let her touch me like that?" Heather screams. "Kill her." She screeches. "Kill her, now!"

I grab hold of Isadora's waist and let the towel drop to the floor right in front of her. My hand reaches around and touches Isadora's belly, then my fingers dance down to her cunt.

Heather makes some sort of screeching sound and shakes her head while attempting to stand.

Isadora's hand reaches for my hair, threading her fingers through it, as I slide a finger in.

"Leave Heather, before I kill *you*."

"You…" she spits. "You *will* pay for this." She points a look at Isadora, but I turn her in my arms as the door is yanked open and Heather leaves with a slam of the door.

"Get your hands off me." Isadora pulls at my hair and steps away, my fingers immediately slipping out of her. I put them to my lips and suck them one by one like lollypops.

"That's not going to happen, Isadora. I can't help myself when it comes to you. Each passing day I'm becoming more and more addicted."

"I'm leaving this place, Jasper. And you can't stop me," she says reaching for the towel and wrapping it around her. When she does, I see the glint of something shiny and I know instantly what it is.

"Pass me the knife, Isadora."

PLAYETTE

Her head shakes but it's slow, and there's a smile of desperation touching her lips.

"I have nothing more to give. Nothing. You and your people took everything from me."

I reach for the knife, she steps back, and with a move I never saw coming, she drop kicks my legs out from under me so I fall to the floor, then her hand comes up to punch me straight in my face.

"Well played, my love. Well played," I whisper as the knife touches my throat.

CHAPTER 20
Isadora

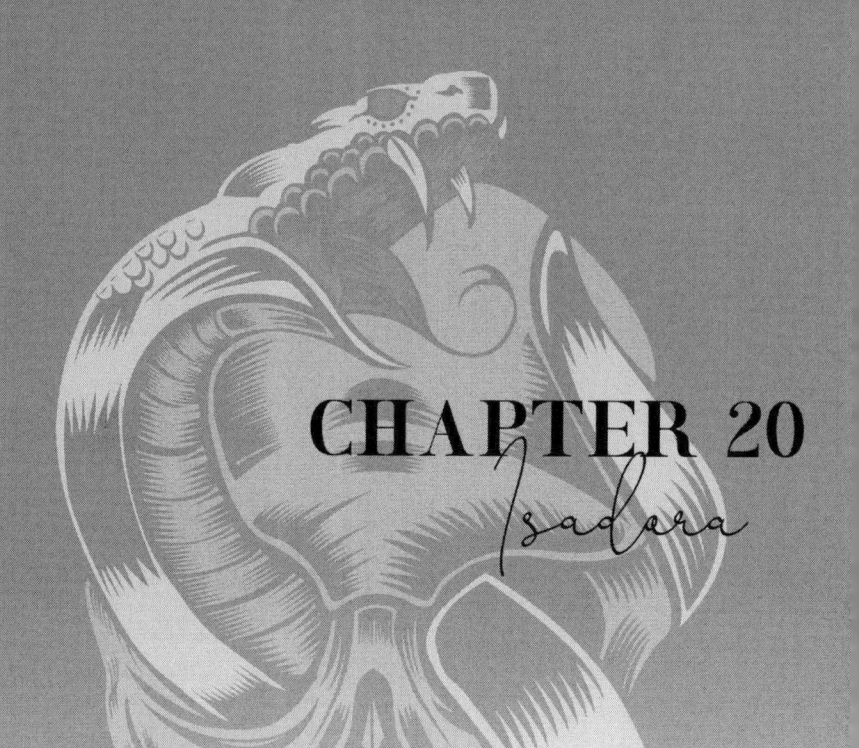

MY HAND GRIPS the knife tightly while Jasper smiles up at me with a sinister smirk, one I've come to love. But it has to be done, I have to do it. I have to end him.

"Do it," he says through blood-coated teeth as he bucks under me and screams in my face. "Do it, Isadora."

A tear leaves my eyes as I know what he's asking from me.

"If you don't, I'll hunt you down and kill you. Is that what you want?"

Fuck! I shake my head while tasting my tears.

We both turn when the door handle moves,

but I don't shift the pressure I have on his neck.

"You've played me well, Isadora. You took what no other woman could. So, I guess the joke's on me?"

What does he mean? I took him, took his men. Arghhh, he's stressing me out.

"Shut up!" Shaking my head at his words while looking back to the door, I'm waiting for someone to walk in.

"How is it possible for you to make me feel this way?"

I grind my teeth at his words. "Shut. Up."

"Do it, Isadora. Fucking do it."

"I hate you," I say with tears flowing down my cheeks now.

"I know… I know you do."

The door opens, and as it does, I apply more pressure until blood starts to bloom. Jasper doesn't move or look like it fazes him one little bit.

"Isadora, you need to do something before Ace shoots you."

I look over to the door and see Ace holding a gun in his hand that's raised directly at my head.

"He's my boss, my law, my life, Isadora. I will put a bullet through your head for him," Ace says.

Even if Ace likes me, he loves and respects Jasper more. He is his king, after all. They live by

PLAYETTE

old fashioned laws of respect — the mafia boss is not to be betrayed nor disrespected.

"He deserves it. Damn it, you all do," I say through gritted teeth.

Jasper chuckles.

I stand, bringing him with me, the knife still in my hand. "I'm walking out of here, and you will *not* follow or stop me."

Jasper pulls himself away from me, shakes his head. My eyes roam him, his blood is trickling over his body but he doesn't care. At all. I'm sure he's had much worse.

"That can't happen, pink," Ace replies.

I back up and keep my eyes on Jasper. Ace is in the room, but away from the door which is where I'm heading.

"It will. Or I'll take my own life before you can."

Jasper's eyes go wide at my words. With the knife in my hand, I lift it to my own neck and begin applying pressure, I feel the sting straight away as I break the skin.

"Isadora..."

"You want me dead. You need me dead. What if I make it easier on you and do it myself?" I ask, wanting to know his value for me. A shiver comes over me as I inhale a shallow breath and take another.

"Remove it from your neck. Now," he seethes.

"I would have killed you, given the chance," I tell him.

He smirks. "You've had plenty of chances, Isadora. Just admit you're feeling what I am and drop the damn knife." He doesn't understand what I'm feeling, I hardly understand my mixed emotions when it comes to him.

A loud noise sounds behind me, and in that moment I take my chance, as everyone is focused on the disturbance. Clutching the towel with one hand and the knife in the other, I run down the stairs two at a time. I notice Carter before he sees me, and as he does, he stands at the same time my hand touches the door handle which leads outside.

"Don't you hurt her," I hear someone yell, but it doesn't slow me as my bare feet hit the asphalt and I take off running. I see a car, the door's open and I run to it, sliding in and thanking God when I see the keys are in the ignition.

"What the fuck?"

Starting the engine, I drive, and that's when I notice Heather who's screeching next to me. I missed the fact she's there and fucking sitting right next to me.

"Shut the fuck up," I yell as I take the exit onto the main road. I check in my rearview mirror to make sure I'm not being followed, and after a few checks my heart rate starts to slow and I can finally breathe again.

PLAYETTE

"They're going to kill you so bad for this," she fumes next to me.

How the fuck did I not see Heather for what she was? I pride myself on my impressions of people, and I totally got this one wrong. What a cunt.

"Possibly," I say pulling over. "Now *you* can get the fuck out."

Heather's eyes go wide. "Fucking hell. It's raining, and cold," she says as if I care.

I look her up and down I order, "Give me your clothes."

Heather shakes her head. "That's not going to happen."

The knife which I placed between my legs is lifted and I push it to her neck. "Honestly? You don't want to fuck with me, bitch. Least of all today, Heather. If that's even your real name. Now give me your fucking clothes before I slit your pretty little throat."

"I just bought this skirt," she whines as she lifts her ass and slides it off. "Benny's car had a tracker, did you know that?"

I didn't.

I had no idea, but I don't tell her that. Though, my uncle had his suspicions.

At least now I know how they found me.

"The shirt, too." She hands me the skirt then pulls the shirt off to reveal a shiny silver bra underneath. "Now… Get. The. Fuck. Out."

Her eyes go wide. "What? No. No way. I'll freeze."

I grab the towel which is covering my body and pull hard then hand it to her. "Get out before I cut your damn throat, Heather."

She crosses her arms over her chest. I lift the knife touching it to her skin, she jumps, her hand quickly clutching at the towel as she gets out.

The minute she is out, I drive off and only quickly pull over briefly to dress so I'm not naked.

"Fuck, fuck, fuck."

I bang on the steering wheel.

I don't know where to go or what to do.

I have to get my uncle out of that place, but to do that I need to have something in return. Getting out, I leave the keys in the ignition and start walking. I can't stay here any longer because if this car has a tracking device on it I'm fucked, and I'll have no chance of getting my uncle back alive. Seeing Heather's phone I make my first call.

"Benny," he answers on the first ring.

"Girl, they have been looking for you," is all he says. I like Benny, and the last thing I want to do is bring him into this bullshit, but I don't know where else to go. I grew up in this area, but I isolated myself so I had no friends, and it was

PLAYETTE

just my uncle and me. He said it was best to keep it that way.

"I need somewhere to go."

"Sharon's," he answers straight off the bat.

"No way. We don't get along."

"Exactly," he states then hangs up. Not long after a text comes through with an address.

Rubbing my arms, I come to a stop out front of a perfectly manicured house. It's small, almost cottage-like, and perfect in every way. I shouldn't be here. But it's the last place they will think to look for me, so my knuckles tap on the door while I try to think of a good excuse.

"Oh, hell no," Sharon says the minute she sees me. "I knew you were trouble. You're in trouble, right?" I nod, not even bothering to lie. What's the point? She looks behind her then back to me before she opens the door letting me in. "Look, you can't stay for long. I know who they are and I can't risk it."

"Mommy." A little girl with blonde curly hair walks up to Sharon and wraps her little arms around Sharon's legs. Sharon leans down and picks her up then places her on her hip.

"You need to go back to sleep. No staying up tonight," Sharon says then looks back to me. "Stay here. Don't touch anything."

I nod and she walks away.

Rubbing my hands up and down my arms, I'm

absolutely freezing even though the room is warm. I look around. *What is this place?* I see photographs of Sharon and the little girl everywhere. *How did I not know this fact?* A three-seater black sofa sits in front of a television with a toy chest in the middle, in the corner where someone would put a bookcase is another toy chest. It's a home you would want to be raised in as a child. It's sweet and above all feels safe, it's something I miss.

"What are you doing here?" Sharon crosses her arms over her chest.

"You have a daughter?" I ask, surprised.

"Yes. Now answer me, please."

"Heather isn't who she says she is."

Sharon rolls her eyes. "Of course, not. She was sucking up your ass so hard I knew she was fake." She walks to her quaint kitchen, opens a top cupboard and pulls out a small Keurig. "Just as I knew you were lying to me about that guy."

"Don't ask me to tell you. You have a little one, Sharon."

She spins and leans on the counter as she watches me. "You're in trouble?"

I nod and she sighs. "You can stay here for the night, on the couch, it's all I can give you. Bella has to go to school in the morning and I have my day job."

"Thank you, Sharon. And sorry..."

PLAYETTE

She shrugs. "I don't get it, even if I want to say I do. But if you were my daughter looking for help, I'd hope someone would do exactly that." She turns around and starts to pour the coffee.

"Where is... where's her dad?"

"He died when she was two months old. It wasn't that long after that I started at the club. I had to. I had absolutely no choice. I need to be able to support us."

"No judgment here, Sharon," I say holding up my hands.

"It's just us, and it's hard. But I do what I can, you know?"

I nod and instantly feel bad for coming here. But I don't know anyone else, and Heather won't think to look here as they all think I hate Sharon.

"Do you need money, Issy?" I shake my head. "Are you sure? You don't have anything on you?"

"I could never take money from you." Her hand slides into her pocket and she pulls out a few bills sliding them over to me.

"It's a loan. You can pay me back when you can."

I nod, putting the cash into my skirt pocket, well, technically, Heather's skirt, then take the coffee she also slides my way.

"If you see anyone... anyone at all, don't tell them you saw me," I tell her.

"Of course."

"Thanks, Sharon."

"Mommy," is called again and Sharon points to the couch. "You can sleep there, blanket and pillow is already on it." She starts to walk off, leaving me sitting at her counter. "And, Issy…" I turn to look at her, "… don't mention what we do."

"Of course."

Sharon walks off to tend to Bella, and then I hear the soft hum of a voice and I know she's singing to her. Maybe I've had her pegged for the wrong type of person after all. Maybe my judgment of character is way off.

Walking over to the couch, I curl myself up into a ball, and when I close my eyes, a man with a scarred lip and fucked-up back is staring at me.

CHAPTER 21
Jasper

"FIND HER," I scream, throwing the nearest thing my hand comes in contact with.

Ace shakes his head. "I could have killed her, boss," he says.

I turn to look at him. "I could have killed you, too," I bark.

"You love her?" He states it, but it's a good question, and a smile forms on his lips like he's just figured something out.

"I do not."

"But you do," he replies.

I run my hand through my hair. "Did I give you permission to talk back to me this way?" I ask, raising my voice.

"Sorry, boss," he says, then steps out of the room.

The door reopens and Carter steps in. "You do love her. You wouldn't hesitate to kill her otherwise."

"I don't know what I feel, but not killing her is not an option right now," I say honestly. It's the truth and that fact confuses me, I've never been in love, and I'm unsure if what I'm feeling for her is that. My emotions are all over the place, but one thing I do know without hesitation, is I don't want her to die. Yet. And that speaks volumes about who I am.

Not many things in this life give me fear, not many things in this life I need.

My fear and my need for her are all very new. And working all that out is proving to be harder than anticipated.

"The uncle is asking to see her," Carter says.

"He can go fuck himself."

"If only that was possible." He chuckles as he walks out.

"Boss, here she is." Ace pushes Heather into the room. She's wearing the towel that I wrapped around Isadora. She holds it up over her chest as her eyes gaze at the floor, waiting for me to speak.

"Where would she go?"

PLAYETTE

"She never told me much. Honestly, I don't know." Heather shrugs her shoulders.

"Think, Heather, think." I reach for a shirt, sliding it on as I wait for her to speak.

"Maybe work. She was always working."

"Why did you let her take your car?" I ask.

Heather's eyes go wide. "I did no such thing. That whore stole it."

I tsk-tsk at her. "Careful with your words, Heather. You are the only whore I see here right now."

"What's so special about her?" she asks.

"Does it matter?"

"Yes."

"She's special… to me. That's all that matters."

"Whatever," she murmurs.

"Leave now, Heather."

"Aren't we going to fuck?"

"*Leave*. Now. Heather."

She makes some sort of sound as she turns and walks out the door. I reach for my phone and dial Isadora's number, it doesn't even ring.

Ace is standing outside the door when I step through.

"Burn all his shit. Strip it down."

He nods as I begin walking down the stairs to a loud scream that soon follows.

The uncle is seated in a chair, tied to it, and a

ball gag hangs from his mouth stopping him from speaking. I pull it from his mouth and he spits on the floor and looks up at me with hate in his eyes. Believe me I detest him just as much.

"Where would she go?"

He smiles. "As if I'd tell you."

Carter hands me an iron poker, one that was hanging on the fire tool set stand right next to the fire. I step over and place it in the flames and wait for a few minutes but continue to talk, "Did you know my mother would burn me? Just small ones, nothing overly large, just enough to leave a scar as a reminder not to anger her again?" I tell him, looking down at the iron poker. "This tool…" I move it around in my hands admiring it, "… she would press it to my skin until I screamed, and when she lifted it off I could smell my own skin burning. That's not something a child should have to deal with, the fear of a mother who physically hurts you. Don't you think?"

"You deserved it."

I raise an eyebrow. "A ten-year-old kid deserves to be burned as punishment for walking down the stairs?" I sigh while shaking my head. Slipping on a protective glove, I pull the iron from the fire and walk over to his chair. Without hesitation I slam it onto his hands which are tied to the back of the chair. I press hard on his skin hearing the sound before I smell the distinct odor

PLAYETTE

of burning flesh. He screams, it's blood-curdling, and as I pull it away some of his skin comes with it and some is left hanging from his hand. "You still think so?"

He nods his head. "She should have killed you." His head rears back. This man is weak, so weak, using a girl to do his dirty work.

"But you know what happened, right? I killed her." I smile, placing the hot iron on his skin again. He screams, and Carter shoves the ball gag back in his mouth to shut him the fuck up. I burn him one more time, just for fun, before we leave.

It doesn't take long to arrive at the club, and when we do, Benny's there as always. He sees us and stands a little taller.

"Have you seen Issy?" Carter asks.

Benny looks to me then back to Carter. "No."

"Do you know where she might have gone?" I ask.

He answers straight away, "She only comes here or home. And she's mostly here. Lately, though, she's been with you."

I nod, looking around.

"What about the last girl she brought to our house?"

"Sharon. Her name was Sharon," Ace says then looks to Benny. "Sharon here?"

"No, she isn't on today. But they hate each other," Benny says with conviction.

"That's true. Issy didn't like her much at all." I smile.

"Where does she live?"

"She wouldn't go there. You obviously don't know Issy at all. She detests Sharon," Heather says walking in overdressed much like she always is. She crosses her arms over her chest. "And Sharon hates her right back," she states.

"You're like a bad smell, aren't you?" I say to her.

Heather scrunches up her nose, turns on her heels and walks away.

I spin back to look at Benny. "That address?"

He shakes his head. "You want me to give you my employee's address?"

I step closer to him. "Technically, she's *my* damn employee. So, yes, I want her address. And make it fast, old man, I have someone I need to catch before she runs."

Benny grumbles something as he steps off to retrieve the information.

I smile, knowing I may just be one step closer to *her*.

It's a small place, the sun is starting to rise. And before I get out of the car Carter places a

PLAYETTE

hand on my chest stopping me. "She has a kid. Possibly three years old. Maybe we should wait?"

And that's what we do, we wait for two hours out the front of this little cottage. I notice movement and decide it's time to pay her a visit.

Knocking on the door, I hear a little girl's laughter followed by Sharon smiling as she opens the door. When she notices me, she quickly tries to slam it shut. But I knew that reaction was coming, so I stop it by putting my foot between the door and the frame.

"Sharon," I say. "I simply want to talk. No need to cause a scene. I'm not here to cause any trouble."

"Momma, who's that?"

"Go to your room and pack your bag, sweetie. You've got school today." I hear little footsteps running before the door is pulled open slightly. Sharon looks me over. "I'm not inviting you in."

I nod, I didn't think she would anyway. I wouldn't invite myself into my own home.

"You know why I'm here, right?"

Sharon crosses her hands over her chest. "No." She holds the door half shut the whole time we speak, not wanting to open it fully.

"Come on, Sharon. You don't want to lie to me, do you?"

Her eyes go wide as if I've just threatened her.

I guess I did.

Kind of.

"Who are you looking for?"

"Now Sharon... that's the thing... I never said I was looking for anyone, now did I?"

"Why else would you be here, at my house?" she asks.

Maybe she isn't so dumb after all.

"Is she here, Sharon?"

"Who?"

Smart girl. "Is Isadora here?"

"Why would she be here? I don't even like her, and she sure as shit hates me."

"But that's the thing though, Sharon, I do. I like her. And when I like something I get very mad when I lose it. You see, I don't lose things often, so when I do I cannot control my temper."

"I think it's time you left," Sharon says, shutting the door.

But before she can shut it fully, I say, "You'll let me know, won't you, Sharon? If you happen to see her? It would be a shame to lose everything you've worked for based on a lie." I turn before she can say another word and walk back to the car, the front door shuts and not long after one of the front curtains start to shift. I notice Sharon poke her head out to see if I'm still here. I offer her a small wave before she quickly snaps the curtain shut.

PLAYETTE

Isadora's in there, I know it.

For two people who hate each other, they're sure doing a good job of protecting one another.

I'll have her back by the end of the night, and maybe then I'll think about her punishment.

CHAPTER 22
Isadora

SHARON'S FACE IS red, she's more than a little freaked out. I can't blame her, I've put her in this situation. I feel absolutely fucking terrible.

"I'll sneak out the back, he'll never know I was here," I say truly remorseful. I should have asked Benny more questions, I shouldn't have brought this to her doorstep. Just because I never liked Sharon doesn't mean I want her dead. But now I understand her a little better I feel as though I should have stayed away.

"Thugs," she cries out while shaking her head. "And to think I wanted to be part of that world. So fucking glad I didn't." She picks up her daughter's backpack, calls her name and then looks at me. "You can stay, but if you do, don't look out the front window, and if you do decide to leave definitely leave out the back. But above all, be damn careful because they are waiting outside."

I nod my head once. "Thank you, Sharon. I will pay you back. I'm sorry." It's all I can say, after all, I have brought danger to her front door.

"You have a lot going on, I realized it from the first moment I saw you. It's why I stayed away. But please, don't bring any more of your shit here." She reaches for her daughter's hand and walks out the front door. I hear her start the car and when it pulls away, it isn't long until I hear footsteps.

"Isadooora... Isadooora," he calls my name, taunting me.

He knows I'm here.

How the fuck he knows, I have no clue.

I'm not friends with Sharon and everyone knows it.

Grabbing a hoodie that Sharon left for me to wear, I step out the back of the house onto the porch. I notice he's walking around, so I quickly and quietly turn and run to the front of the house opening the door. I see Ace sitting in the car, I smile as I clasp the knife I have in my hand. I can hear Jasper calling my name, and it's like a lullaby the devil would sing to you. One you want to go to, one you're seduced by, but you

PLAYETTE

know damn well you shouldn't be. Ace is tapping his fingers on the steering wheel when I open the passenger door, I slide in next to him.

"Fuck." Ace goes to move his hand to his belt, but before he can use his knife I have mine slamming into his hand, going in deep until I hit the car seat springs. He grunts loudly. I smile that he didn't cry out in pain because it's got to hurt. Honestly, I thought he would scream blue murder, but for some reason he's quiet. It's not something I wanted to do, I like him, but I still have a mission and he's one of those who should be dead. I've failed on that account, too.

"Press down on the gas. Now."

He shakes his head, his teeth grinding together, my hand staying on the knife through his hand and I twist. He grunts a little louder this time. "Drive. Now."

He presses on the gas as I turn around to see Jasper standing in the middle of the road with a smile on his face. It's not a nice smile, more like a smirk, but I can see he's more than fucked off through his gritted teeth.

He's angry, a shiver wracks through my body as I turn around in my seat not wanting to think what he will do to me if he catches me right now. That thought scares me.

"What the fuck are you doing, pink?"

Turning around in my seat. "Take a left." He

does. "Right."

"Pink…" he warns using his nickname for me. "He'll find you. I've never seen Jasper so fixated on someone like he is on you."

"Good for him." I pull the knife out of his hand and he grunts loudly.

"Why haven't you done it? Why haven't you killed him? That's what you're meant to do, right? Kill Jasper?"

I laugh at him. "I'm meant to kill you all," I say wiping the knife blade on the seat.

"Why haven't you killed me, then?"

I don't lie when I answer, "I was planning to."

He turns and looks at me, surprised. "Would you have done it?"

I nod my head. "Yes, it was just a matter of time."

"I don't believe you."

I shrug. "Lucky for me, I don't care what you think."

He starts laughing. "Your uncle's a real piece of work."

"Where is he?" I demand. I need him back, and I will do anything in my power to make sure it happens.

"Where you left him, still at the mansion."

"Pull over."

He does so. As soon as the car is stopped I take the keys from the ignition, burst out of the

PLAYETTE

passenger side and walk around to the driver's side. "I'm guessing this car has a tracker, too?"

He nods his head. "Of course, it does."

"Lift your hands above your head, if you move I'll stab you." I reach for the gun tucked into his belt.

"I couldn't kill you even if I tried, pink."

"Why is that?"

"The boss won't allow it."

"How sweet," I say, rolling my eyes while stepping back. Jasper, with all his hearts and flowers, maybe he should really start sending them instead of telling his men not to kill me.

"It is when you think about it. I know what he would do to you if he didn't care. If you were just another bitch. I'm going to tell you, pink, because he is, make no mistake, a ruthless fucking killer. The last bitch who thought they had a chance with him ended up in a body bag and sent back to her parents' doorstep. But you have no parents to be sent back to, isn't that right, pink?"

He's right, my parents are dead and it's all because of who they are and what they are. I loved them without a shadow of a doubt, and because of them I'm here in this very moment right now. Or, correction, I am here because Jasper chose not to kill me. I shake my head, not wanting to think of that.

"He could try to kill me, but I don't think he

will. Maybe I'll find a way for him to kill all of you first. What do you think he would say if I told him you touched me?"

"Clever. Clever girl." Ace shakes his head. "I can see why he likes you. But remember, pink, a zebra can't change their stripes."

I slide back into the car and we start driving back to the mansion. Ace's phone, which is next to me, starts ringing. Jasper's face appears, so I answer it.

"They'll kill you, Isadora, the minute you step out of that car."

"You better hope they don't then because I'm pulling up into your driveway right now. Goodbye, lover." I hang up the phone, and as I pull up closer to the house, I notice Carter standing on the front steps with the phone to his ear.

Stepping out of the car, I shut the door with a knife in one hand and the gun in the other.

Carter hangs up, shakes his head as he slides his hands into his pockets.

"Who would have thought, a girl with pink hair would make my boss lose all train of logical thought."

"Must be some magical pussy, right?" I joke with him, but my hands never leave either of my weapons.

"Must be," he murmurs. "If you come in here,

PLAYETTE

Isadora, I will prevent you from leaving. And you will not be taking your uncle with you."

"I came for him. I *will* be taking him."

"Why so selfless with him? He doesn't give two shits about you."

"You don't know that."

I take the first step, then the second, until I'm standing in front of Carter. "He gave you orders not to kill me, correct?"

"Correct." I step past him and inside the mansion. Shit, it stinks. It didn't smell like this when I left. I scrunch up my nose and screw my eyebrows together. "Oh, that smell… that's your uncle's skin. Stinks, right?" He chuckles.

I turn fast and shoot, Carter drops to the floor hard and fast, his hands clutching at his leg where the bullet went through.

"Hurts, right?" I laugh while walking past him. My uncle's tied to a black chair, his eyes are shut and his hands are badly burned.

"Uncle."

He lifts his head and looks at me, shakes it, and pulls on his restraints. I still hear Carter whinging and swearing from where I left him in the main entryway.

"Untie me. Fast."

I slide the gun into my skirt and start to untie my uncle. He smells, bad. Burned skin and body flesh is an acrid smell, one I honestly don't want to have to encounter again. I have to remember to breathe through my mouth instead of my nose as I move to the other side untying him.

"Did they do anything else to you?"

He shakes his head as footsteps come into view.

Jasper's standing there with a hard look on his face, as he looks from me to my uncle.

"That's two men you've injured today, Isadora."

I shrug.

Jasper wipes at his lips. "I'll have to kill him now. You've brought this on yourself."

"No, you won't. And if you do, Jasper... I will kill *you*."

"You wouldn't."

I stand in front of my uncle as he stands. "I would with no hesitation. Make no mistake, I will be saving the last standing member of my family, if I have to."

"Who do you think took your parents in the first place?" Jasper asks, his head dropping to the side.

"You and your people."

Jasper chuckles. "You really did brainwash her, didn't you? Does it make you happy to make her your little combat toy?" Jasper questions, looking behind me. I'm confused by his words and what they mean.

PLAYETTE

"You don't know what you're talking about," my uncle says from behind me.

"Oh, but I do. I remember it all, Max."

I turn to my uncle.

How could Jasper know his name?

"What's he talking about?"

"Nothing. Remember, they're all liars. You know better than to trust them."

"I don't," I say.

"You shouldn't trust him either, Isadora."

I turn back to Jasper, who pulls out a photograph and turns it around to show me. Stepping one step closer, but not close enough to touch it, but close enough so I can see the picture, I gasp.

That's my uncle.

And that's his mother.

Jasper's mother.

Turning around, my uncle looks angry. Extremely angry. "How dare you."

"Was she a whore for you, too?" Jasper teases.

"You don't get to speak of her, you evil spawn," my uncle yells.

"But I do. Just because you were fucking her, don't think you were the only man who was at the time."

"You know nothing."

"She was still fucking my father up until I

T.L. SMITH

killed her."

I gasp at his words, shocked by all of it. This can't be real. None of what he's saying is true. It can't be. But Jasper doesn't tell lies either, he's a straight talker. And my uncle? I turn to face him. "This isn't true, right?" I say looking directly at my uncle.

Carter walks in, his leg bandaged, as Ace follows behind with his hand covered in a bandage as well.

"She wasn't." My uncle sneers looking at Jasper and ignoring what I've just asked him.

"Oh, but she was." He laughs.

"How does it feel knowing I also fuck your niece? I bet that burns a little bit, right? Knowing the woman you loved used you," Jasper says making me wonder what the hell is going on.

"Shut the fuck up," my uncle screams, then turns to me with a crazy look in his eyes. "We need to leave. Kill them," he orders me as if I wasn't just standing here listening to all of this.

I shake my head. "Is what he's saying true? You were with her?" I ask my uncle not sure who to believe right at this moment though the photo is more than enough evidence.

"Of course I was, she was it for me."

Oh fucking hell! I gasp at his words. "Why didn't you tell me?"

"She was sick, so fucking sick," Jasper says,

PLAYETTE

shaking his head. "She should've been locked up."

"No, you tried that. I got her out," Uncle Max says as if he's proud of himself.

"I wonder what else she's made you do." Jasper thinks, but it's out loud.

"None of your fucking business." He turns to me. "Isadora, we're leaving. Now." He attempts to reach for my hand, but I pull it back.

Jasper's standing closest to me, and looks at me with clear intent written in his eyes. "Don't leave with him."

"You'll just kill me when you're sick of me," I say, shaking my head.

"No, I won't, Isadora. And you know that."

"No. No, I don't," I say, turning to look at my uncle. "Why didn't you tell me?"

"You didn't need to know that fact. I had to keep you on the straight and narrow. You had one task, and one task only… to get rid of them all."

"She did need to know it," Jasper replies.

Ace and Carter stay back, just right of the door, not moving, simply watching.

"There's a lot you've kept from her. Don't you think it's time you told her?"

"Shoot him, Isadora."

"No," I say, stepping back away from my uncle with scrunched hands and my eyebrows so pulled together I'm sure it's now formed one brow.

"Isadora…" I turn to face Jasper, his lips are in a thin line as he stares at me. "You can stay. Please stay."

I want to, but another part of me doesn't.

Everything's a lie.

How much more is a lie.

Did they even kill my parents? Or was I made to believe that by Uncle Max as well?

"No, she will not. You can't have her."

I feel it then, the gun that's tucked into my skirt is now in the hands of my uncle. And it's raised high to meet Jasper's head who's standing directly in front of me. "Your mother should have done this a long time ago, you evil piece of shit."

It all happens so fast.

The gun clicks.

Jasper flies backward.

I see the impact and I'm hopeless to stop it.

Jasper falls to the floor.

My whole body starts shaking and my eyes form tears I didn't know were there as I drop to the floor next to him. "Jasper." I touch his face, but I'm pulled backward.

Hands grab my shoulders and when I pull back something sharp hits the back of my head, and soon, I succumb to the blackness.

CHAPTER 23
Isadora

I WAKE TO hear screaming as I'm carried out.

"Fix your boss and fucking move," my uncle seethes.

Fuck, my head hurts and it's even more painful to open my eyes.

"Leave her."

"No can do. She isn't yours and you won't get her. I'll kill her before I let you mongrels have her." My uncle begins walking me out of the house, my hands push against his back and he puts me down to the ground. "Get in, Isadora, I'll explain later."

My head starts shaking, but he doesn't wait for

me to speak as he pushes me in roughly. I look for Jasper. My heart is on the ground, shattered, but filled with mixed emotions, ones I can't begin to understand. Carter's on the ground next to him, but I don't have a clear view. Ace is standing out front watching with his gun raised as my uncle climbs in and starts the engine. It's one of Jasper's cars, so I know it will be tracked which I don't tell my uncle.

I'm not really sure what's going on anymore, so best to keep that little fact a secret right now.

"Did you use me?" I ask while rubbing my head. "Did you even love me as your niece?" I need to know, was all this a lie to him? I love him. I will always love him. It hurts to know he might not feel the same. He is my only family.

"I did use you. They took everything I loved."

"What about me?" I cry while my hands pull through my hair in frustration.

The fucker bangs his hands on the wheel. "What about you, Issy? Not everything is about you. I spent a good portion of my life training you to be the woman you are today, and yet you still fell for him? Why? Why would you do that? How could you do that? After all that training, after all that deceit, you still fell for a man that you thought killed your family."

"Who said I've fallen for him?"

He scoffs. "Please. I know the look of love, I've had it. It makes you do crazy shit. This is why

PLAYETTE

you must leave him."

"Or what?"

He turns to look at me. "You don't want the answer to that question, Issy. Trust me."

"But I do. What would you do if I said I wanted to go back to him?" Because I do. I really do. I know I want Jasper.

"I will kill you," he says so easily.

"You would?" I ask him.

"Yes, Issy, I would. They're vile, imbecilic bastards."

"From what I heard, his mother was worse."

When he turns to look at me, anyone would think I've just killed his dog. "No, she was not," he says with a voice full of anger.

"She tortured Jasper," I scream.

"He deserved it," he replies, driving back to the garage.

I balk at his words. For fuck's sake. *He can't mean that, right?*

"How could a ten-year-old boy possibly deserve to be tortured that way? Have you seen his back?"

"Because he was *his* child."

"No. No way. That's not fair to a child." I shake my head.

"It is. He is evil spawn, and all who come from that man should and will die."

231

"I don't hate him."

He coughs. "No, you silly girl. You fucking love him. But I'll change that. He won't get you like he got her."

"Why did she leave?" I ask, trying to work this all out.

"He killed her."

"I know that, but why was she with him? She had to have left you, right? I mean to be back there?"

"You don't know what you're talking about." He comes to a stop out the front of his garage and gets out walking to my door. "Move it. They know about this place, so we don't have long." He carries the gun in his hand as he steps inside. "Grab the rifle, and go up to the roof."

He hands me the gun, but I just look at it, confused. "No," I say, shaking my head.

"Issy, now is not the time to have a change of heart. They're coming here to kill us both."

"Not me," I say, holding the rifle firmly in my grasp.

"Yes, maybe not you, but definitely me. Do you want them to kill the only family you have left?"

A loud crashing noise vibrates through me, and the car we stole smashes through the front of the garage.

"What are you doing? Run."

PLAYETTE

I drop the rifle to the floor as they walk in. I look around for Jasper but don't see any sign of him. My heart deflates at that thought, because that means something, right? Maybe what my uncle said is true. Maybe I do love him. Maybe.

Ace steps over to me, wraps his hand around my upper arm and starts pulling me away. "Where is he?"

I look around to see if I can see my uncle but he's nowhere. Guess, he's in hiding right about now, but even after everything I still don't want them to kill him. I don't know everything about what's going on in my messed up life, but I do know that.

"You're coming with us." Ace pulls on my arm and yanks me out to the car. I see Jasper lying on the back seat with his eyes shut.

"He's all right, right?"

"I don't know. We're taking him to our doctor." His breathing is heavy and slow and it's more than a little concerning. I climb in the back with him and move his head, so it's lying on my lap. When I look up, Carter and Ace are staring at us.

"You really fucked him up, didn't you?" Carter asks but it's more of a statement. Carter shakes his head and then looks back to Ace as he climbs in the passenger seat.

"I didn't know."

"There's a lot you don't know. Maybe next time you should ask," Ace grumbles as Carter starts driving erratically fast. I don't look back as we leave the garage, but I know my uncle will know I've left with them. And I'm afraid of what he might do.

"He's bleeding… a lot."

"Put pressure on it," Carter says as I touch Jasper's chest.

Blood starts to pool through the cloth and over my hand.

"You better fucking hope he doesn't die. He's your pass to staying alive."

"Fuck you." I lean down to Jasper's face, touch my lips to his forehead as we come to a stop.

What have I done?

A man and a woman step out from an old house with latticework that's falling off and simply dangling there. The place is on acres of land all by itself, there's no other houses or anyone in sight. Quickly opening the back door, the man looks at me then to Jasper. Pulling him free from the car, he carries him inside the house.

"Whose place is this?" I ask.

"The doc's." The answer is simple, but I get the meaning.

We follow behind and Ace pushes his hand out, stopping me as we arrive at the open door. "Maybe you should stay outside."

PLAYETTE

I shake my head.

He shrugs, so I follow him into the room.

A scream rips through the room and I run in after it. Jasper's awake, his shirt's been torn off as the doctor works on his wound. Carter's holding him in place so he can't move.

"Why aren't you numbing him? Give him anesthetic?" I ask.

Jasper looks to me. "I don't want it." Then he passes out anyway.

Carter removes his hands from Jasper and the doctor continues his work.

It's quiet, the only sound in the room is the instruments being picked up and placed in a steel kidney dish, and of course, people breathing.

My hand squeezes hard while I watch and I lose all my breath. *What have I done?*

There's blood everywhere and Jasper's completely out of it.

CHAPTER 24
Jasper

SHE'S STANDING NEXT to me when I wake, her hand is on my arm holding me in place as her head lays on the bed. I move my fingers and touch her hair which causes her to stir then she sits up fast, almost falling from her chair. I look around and see that I'm back in my room, my shoulder's fucking aching, and Carter's sitting near the door with a gun in one hand and his phone in the other.

"You're awake." She startles. "You've woken up before, but you keep passing out," she says nervously.

"I see you're still alive," I say attempting to sit up, so she moves a pillow behind me so I can, and breathes heavily as she waits.

"I…" she steps back, fear is evident in her eyes, and her hands are shaking.

"If I wanted you dead, Isadora, you'd be dead."

She nods her head. "I didn't know… about your mother, I mean."

"I figured," I say as she passes me a glass of water. I attempt to drink it before she takes it back.

"How did you know?"

"I remember you." She looks at me with her eyebrows drawn which forms a small line across her forehead. "When you were fourteen. I remember you from that day in the shop."

Her eyes go wide. "You were there?"

I nod, it's not a day I want to remember. That was the day I finally knew my father had to be killed. I had become an adult and was now in his world, it was when I grew up. But that day? Yeah, that day was different. He wasn't killing for reason anymore he was killing because he enjoyed it. That was not a man who should be running an empire.

"Why?"

"Your uncle's a liar."

"I don't understand." She shakes her head back and forth while running her hand through her long hair, tears are leaking from her beautiful

PLAYETTE

eyes and it takes everything in me to not touch her. Despite everything, I want her with a force so fierce I can't even contend with it.

"My mother didn't love your uncle, she used him. It's what she did. Used people and discarded them, and she was good at it. It's part of the reason I can smile at you even when I want to kill you."

Carter stands, walks over and hands me some pain medication as Isadora gives me the glass of water.

"You can go."

Carter looks to her then back to me.

"She would have spiked the water if she wanted me dead. Wouldn't you, Isadora?" She doesn't look up, instead she looks down at the floor as Carter nods and walks away.

"Your family's business was profitable. Your uncle was a jealous son of a bitch. They had what he wanted. So for him to get ahold of everything, he asked my mother to have them killed. She persuaded my father to do it. That was easy for her, because at the end he'd do anything for her. He started to live for the highs. This world is dangerous and he had no one to tell him what he was doing was wrong and my mother sure as shit didn't care."

Tears fall from her eyes.

"They died because he was jealous." She

whispers, the truth in her words finally working out the real reason why they died. Even if my father was the one to pull the trigger, it was her uncle who loaded that gun. "Do you?"

"Do I what?" She looks up and wipes the tears.

"Do you have someone to tell you when you're doing wrong?"

"I do. Carter and Ace are my men. They keep me on the straight and narrow. Gabe was, too—"

She hiccups loudly at the mention of his name, interrupting me. "I was angry. I wanted you all dead. It was what I was told and I'm sorry."

"Death is what I'm used to, Isadora. The only issue I've had with death is you." Her hands fall into her lap as I continue, "Your parents business was to be split once your uncle got it between him and my mother."

"What did your mother say to make them do it?"

"You didn't have to tell my father much by then, he would have killed the doorman and laughed as he did it. He had no care factor at all."

"So, she took advantage of that fact."

"It's what she did."

"And then?"

"I remember walking in, your father saying you were closing, and then my father pulling out a gun. You gasped, I grabbed hold and pulled

PLAYETTE

you back and told you to run."

"What would have happened if I'd stayed?"

"You were also marked to be killed, Isadora. Your uncle wanted you dead, too."

"He didn't." She sighs as the realization hits her regarding the truth of it all.

"Everything was left to you. You know this."

I do. I ended up with the money when I turned legal age. "He could have killed me. He knew how. It doesn't make sense."

"It wasn't long after that I took my mother's life," I tell her the truth.

"So, he used me as retaliation," she finally says. "I was his weapon for you taking his love away."

"She didn't love him though, she stopped seeing him, and then I took her."

"You killed her though, right? You told me that," she questions me.

But my eyes become heavy, and I pass out.

CHAPTER 25
Isadora

"SO, YOU'RE LIKE a slut?" Ace says as I walk into the mansion after Jasper had fallen asleep a few hours ago.

I turn to face him. "What?"

"You like to fuck, right?"

"What's that got to do with anything?" I ask, confused and maybe a little taken aback.

"Doesn't that make you a slut?"

Oh, for fuck's sake, I wave him off and flip him the finger. Opening the fridge, Carter walks up and takes a seat next to Ace. Looking down, I see their hands and the small tattoo that I've come to loathe over the years, the one I was trained to kill for.

"How was it... killing them?" Ace questions then shovels food into his face. "I mean, I would like to know. I know Mack was an asshole." He turns, looks to Carter. "Sorry, bro." Then, he faces me again.

"Where's the eggs?" I ask, not answering.

"Maybe you and he will have fucked-up babies together," Ace continues. "Your uncle is fucked, you know. Wanting to kill his own family so he can take their business, and have money to hold on to the girl. The girl who didn't even fucking want him." He chuckles to himself. "Men go crazy for special pussy."

"Will you... Shut. The. Fuck. Up," I say, turning around.

"I bet you were a real momma and daddy's girl, too."

"Remember that knife in your hand? Want another one?" I ask him looking down at his bandaged hand. "Because right now, I would have no hesitation in jamming that knife right into the same hole."

"Please, you caught me off guard. I wouldn't allow you to do that again."

"Who do you care for most in this world, Ace? Is it yourself?"

"Why? Do you want to kill them, too?"

I shrug. "Maybe."

PLAYETTE

"Well, that would be Jasper. So go at it. Kill him, and see how far you get."

"Why?" I ask him.

"Why, what?"

"Why is he the one?"

Ace places his cup on the table and turns to Carter before he looks back to me.

"Jasper's earned our respect. Not just because he's our leader, but because of who he is and what he has been through. You will not find another man as ruthless and as cunning as Jasper in your life. It's him you want at your side in life. It's him you want at your side when you're on your death bed. We were raised to treat our boss with respect, and his word is law. As some have a god, we have Jasper. He is our religion and we will abide by his scripture," Ace says proudly.

"What if you fall in love?"

"Love is second in our world, our world is first. It was the same for our parents, and their parents before them."

"So, like someone who's been brainwashed their whole life, it's like that?" I ask them raising an eyebrow.

Ace leans forward while Carter smirks. "Like you, you mean? By that crazy uncle of yours? Jasper doesn't kill without reason. I can tell you there is always a reason. It's why in the last forty years we're the richest and most successful men in the business."

"What about the sacrifices you have to take and make to get there?"

They both shrug.

"If boss deems it necessary, it's done. No questions. No lies."

"You really do love him."

They both nod.

I look to Carter. "More than your own brother?"

He nods. "More so, if you had killed him instead," he shakes his head. "You wouldn't be standing here now, would you?"

"He was a bad man," I say, remembering him.

"That's why Jasper kept him here, so he couldn't cause trouble."

I look down, feeling terrible for all the things I've done. I shouldn't have done them. But the evidence was there. Or so I thought. The evidence was me. I saw it happen, I just didn't know the circumstances behind it. I wish I had because things would be different right now. My emotions wouldn't be all over the place trying to process the lies and separate them from the truth. It's hard when someone you love your whole life tells you one thing and you find out another. I know who I believe—Jasper—but if I could choose it would be my uncle. If the circumstances were different that is. But they aren't, and he is a

PLAYETTE

liar and he manipulated me to get what he wanted—his revenge. I was just a pawn in his story. Granted, I would like to kill the person responsible for taking my parents from me, but someone already did that.

Jasper, killed his own father, pity he didn't do it sooner. Perhaps before that afternoon when he walked into my parents' shop and shot them dead without a care in the world.

I start making some breakfast for Jasper, ignoring the boys as they whisper to themselves. Just before I go to leave, Carter stops me.

"You should leave, you know. Make it easier."

I ignore his words of warning and keep walking.

When I step out to Jasper's house he's awake and sitting up in his bed watching me as I walk in the door. "I need to get up."

I put the tray down and go to help him, but he waves me off and stands by himself. "My legs aren't injured," he spits, walking over to the table.

I step away from him.

Jasper sits at the table, looks down to the food, then back to me. "You should go."

"But..." I have nothing to say.

"Go, Isadora. Now."

Turning around, I grab my jacket, pulling it on. I walk to the door, stop and wait, hoping he doesn't want me to go, but he doesn't look my way again.

I leave and he doesn't stop me.

My place is clean, Gabe's blood is nowhere to be found. How that's even possible I don't know. The place is exactly as I left it, even down to the clothes I wore before I left sitting on my bed. I walk over to grab the burner phone I have stored in the drawer for when I have to speak to my uncle, and find it has several missed calls registering on the screen.

Calling him, he answers on the first ring. "I knew you'd come to your senses," he says. "Issy?"

"I can't believe you," I say, tears falling from my eyes. "You did it all for her, all of it. You killed my parents for *her*."

He's silent, and that's all the answer I need.

"What? Cat got your tongue?"

"You don't understand. Don't let him brainwash you, Issy."

"That was your job, right?" I laugh, shaking my head and swiping at the tears. "You did that all by yourself."

"No. No, I didn't."

"So, you're saying you didn't have her arrange to kill my family and myself, so you could take the business?"

PLAYETTE

He goes silent.

Again.

And I know the next words that will come from his mouth are a lie. "No, I didn't."

I collapse on my bed, close my eyes, and hang up the phone. I need to get out of here. I need to leave.

After packing my things I slide into my car and drive to Sharon's. I owe her for helping me out when she didn't have to.

Knocking on her door, not long passes and she opens it. Appearing startled to see me, she quickly glances past me to make sure no one else is there before she opens it, fully letting me inside.

"I'm not here to stay."

"I would hope not." She crosses her hands over her chest. "I don't need that in my life, Issy. Those men, I don't want them anywhere near Bella or me."

I hold up my hands. "I get it. I absolutely do." Reaching in my pocket, I pull out some cash and hand it to her. She looks at it, but doesn't take it. "For you, as a thank you."

"No. I don't want your money."

"I owe you for letting me stay, and for putting you in danger."

She shakes her head. "No, you don't. Keep your money. Bella and I are doing fine by ourselves. Thank you."

"Can I ask? Where are your parents?"

She laughs. "Around."

Well, okay, didn't expect that answer.

"Look, Issy, I hope you sort out whatever it is you're running from. But I'm going to have to ask you to leave in case they come looking for you. I don't want that near my house ever again."

I nod. "I just wanted to thank you. You didn't have to do what you did. And I was hoping this money will help you and Bella." I offer her the money again and she shakes her head.

"I don't want it, Issy, and honestly, I'm glad I was able to help."

There's a loud knock on the door and she walks out to open it. "Issy," she calls, and when I walk to the door Ace is standing there.

"Time for you to come home, pink."

"I've only been gone a few hours," I complain.

He shrugs. "Boss' orders."

"Issy," Sharon says, turning to me. "You have to go, and don't come back. Please." I nod, walking past and leaving the cash on the counter by the door as I go.

The minute I'm out the front, Sharon shuts the door, and Ace chuckles. "She ain't fond of us, now is she?"

"No, you scare her. She has a little girl."

He nods. "I know."

PLAYETTE

I climb into his car and see Carter's already in the one I took from their house, starting it up, and pulling out onto the road.

"That changed him, you know? What happened to your parents… it changed him."

"I didn't know."

"He spoke of you as a child and how scared you were, and how evil his father was."

"You were there when he killed him?"

He shrugs. "Yes, I wasn't in the room. But I was in that mansion. He came down with a look on his face like he realized what he'd just done was about to change everything. And it did. The men whom were before us had no qualms about raping and murdering when they wanted. They simply didn't care about anything. Jasper can kill, don't get me wrong. But he does it for the business' sake, and to keep people in line. It's why he's succeeded for so long. Why he's stayed at the top with no one threatening to take him down or remove him from power. All of his men respect and honor him both as a person and a boss."

We stay quiet for the rest of the drive. When we arrive at the mansion, I walk in the door and over to the ten men who are here, who are mostly standing with only a few sitting. I look back to Ace, but he doesn't give me any explanation, he simply nods his head to the door leading to the kitchen where we were this morning.

I spot Jasper first. All the men are now standing as I step inside. Two men are speaking closer to Jasper and are whispering in his ear as he looks up at me. He looks fresh, clean, as if he wasn't just shot.

He stands, his hands dropping to his sides as he looks me over. I've changed, because I didn't think I'd be coming back here again.

"Isadora," he says my name and I melt just a little. "Follow me." He starts walking, and I take tentative steps following until we reach a door. He pulls out a key, opens it, and steps down the stairs. I look down, confused, and wonder what's going on. "Isadora." I'm hesitant, but I take the first step, following him. Each step creeks under my feet until a bright light comes on, and Jasper's standing at the bottom of the steps with his hand outstretched waiting for me.

Stepping into him, he takes my hand in his and squeezes tightly.

"Are you okay?" I ask him, confused by this situation I now find myself in.

"I think I love you, Isadora. Tell me… how does that make you feel?"

I'm shocked by his words. "Quite simply… scared," I tell him the truth. Everything I wanted and worked toward no longer exists. I no longer know what I want in this life.

PLAYETTE

He nods. "Good. Now you can feel what I've been feeling. I don't like it. I don't even know you. Only what you show me, and that's been limited. But now I want you to know me, Isadora." He steps away, his hand staying in mine as he pulls me, and I follow until we reach a solid door. His eyes stare back at me before he reaches for another key, placing it into the lock and turning it with a heavy click. When he turns the key, all I can hear is a loud noise and I go to take a step back, but Jasper keeps a firm hold on my hand.

"What's in there?"

He turns back to look at me. "The other woman I loved."

What the fuck! My heart starts beating erratically as he pulls me in, and I look to where his eyes are pointed. A woman with dull brown hair sits on a bed, her eyes lost as she looks up to the ceiling which is covered in glowing light stars which have been stuck to the ceiling.

"Who is that?"

When she turns at the sound of my voice, she smiles. It's a beautiful, but scary smile.

And I know exactly who this is.

His mother.

"You told me you killed her." I turn to face him with my eyes wide in shock.

"I did. In all the ways that matter to her." He

turns, walking in, stepping next to his mother and leaning down to whisper in her ear. Her eyes find mine and she smiles. "She's sick. Schizophrenia is the diagnosis."

"And you keep her locked down here?" I ask, looking around.

It appears like she has everything she needs—toilet, shower—just no interaction with people.

"He does keep me locked up. Isn't he an evil little spawn. I knew he was evil the minute I laid eyes on him." His mother touches his face, her nails drawing a line down his cheek. "See this…" her finger touches the scar on his lip, "… he was naughty one day, so he had to be punished."

"She did that to you?" I ask, shocked.

"I did a lot of things, but this…" she drags her finger along it once more, "… was nothing in comparison." Then she touches his face once more, then drops her hand to her side.

"Does anyone else know?" I ask.

"Yes, the boys all know. No one else, though."

"So, they play along with you killing her?"

"They do what I say, when will you learn this?"

I turn to look at his mother, who rolls her eyes at his words. "Just like his father, that one. I loved that man, did you know? Jasper, though, he was a mistake. A big mistake. Needed to get rid of him. Should have gotten rid of him." She smacks

PLAYETTE

his chest and he winces.

Shit, his wound.

"Are you okay?" I ask, stepping up to him. I look at his shoulder, but he turns so I can't see.

"Oh, so you care for this spawn." She maniacally laughs. "You are one silly woman." She rolls her eyes.

Ignoring her I ask, "Why? Why did you keep her alive?" It makes no sense to me.

"I love her. She's my mother. I will always love her. I told you." Jasper gives her some pills and she takes them, then pokes her tongue out at him after she's done. It's obviously a routine they have in place.

"I'm sorry," I say while shaking my head.

"Momma," he asks, dropping his head to her level. "Tell me about Max."

CHAPTER 26
Jasper

ISADORA LOOKS TO me. "Will she even remember him?" she asks.

"I don't know, only one way to find out."

"Momma, Max."

Momma scrunches up her nose. "That awful little man… he wanted me to kill his family, so he could be rich and make me happy. What a silly man. Money doesn't make me happy. Hell no. Power does." She cackles then looks to Isadora. "You want my boy because of his power, right?"

"No," Isadora answers without hesitation.

"Max wanted that little girl dead as much as I wanted you dead. It's funny, right?" She throws her head back and laughs, then lies back on her single bed. I get up knowing she's done for the day, and reach for Isadora, taking her back up the stairs and away from her. When I turn to lock the door so no one can go down there, Isadora's standing behind me, her hands by her side, her green eyes lost in thought.

"I'm sorry." She covers her mouth as tears start welling in her eyes. "I'm so fucking sorry." She shakes her head as Carter walks into the room. Her having sympathy for me, is something I have never experienced. No one's cared that deeply for me before that they'd cry because of my situation. Not with the conviction she does. Carter stays behind her and she doesn't notice him because her eyes are now covered by her hands as she tries to wipe away the tears, but he nods his head and walks back out. I step up, placing my hand on her shoulder, a pain shoots through my chest but I don't let it show. I've never had to comfort someone before, and I really don't know how. My mother never needed it, and my father didn't show any sort of affection.

"Isadora."

She continues to sob, but a hiccup leaves her as she does. "I... I killed y-your m-men. Your men. Because of h-him," she stutters out.

"People die, Isadora. It's our way of life."

She looks up, her eyes red and swollen. "How

PLAYETTE

c-can you say t-that?" She shakes her head and composes herself. "If I could bring my parents back, I would. It damn near killed me to lose them."

"And Max knew that, and that's what he used." I pull her to me and try not to make a sound when she lays her head on my chest over my wound.

"I'd understand, you know, if you want me dead."

"I thought about that, even tried to do it," I say smiling while running my fingers through her soft, sensuous hair. "It seems I can't do it. And it seems, I won't let anyone else do it either."

"We have issues," she says through a laugh which is forced, before she pulls her head back. "Oh my God, you're bleeding." Her hands touch my shirt buttons and she pulls at it trying to open them to see where.

"It's fine, Isadora."

She shakes her head. "It's not. It's really not. He wanted you dead, and he's a perfect shot usually."

Reaching for her hand, I take it in mine. "I plan to kill him. You know that, right?"

"Yes. Yes, I do." She nods. "He lied to me, all my life."

"He loved my mother, and I can understand why."

She looks up at me with those lost eyes. "My feelings for you are scrambled, Jasper. I don't know what I feel, but more importantly, after all these years, is how to feel."

I nod. I get it. Doesn't mean I don't understand what I feel. It took me a while, but I know exactly how I feel about Isadora. "Let's go to bed, I need some rest."

"I was leaving." She pulls back from me, her hands cross over her chest as she rubs them.

"Where do you intend to go?"

She shrugs. "Away from this shitty town... just somewhere else."

"Maybe tomorrow we can talk about where you want to go. Tonight, though, let's rest."

Isadora nods and places her hand back in mine as we walk through the mansion and out to my house. As soon as we are inside, she looks around as I walk to the bed and start removing my shirt, which has blood all over it.

"You're still bleeding." She reaches for the first aid kit and pulls out a new bandage and some other cleaning gear and walks toward me. Her hands are gentle as she touches me and cleans my wound, placing the new bandage on carefully. I lean in and place my lips to hers when she pulls her hands away. "Do you think we should?" she asks, her hands moving to the top of my jeans. "We shouldn't," she answers her own question, but doesn't remove her fingers from the zipper.

PLAYETTE

"We so should." I grab hold of her face and kiss her hard, she opens, allowing me in as my tongue dances with hers. I grunt as she leans on me, and she quickly pulls back, her eyes roaming over me.

"I've hurt you. I can't hurt you." She shakes her head and before she steps away, I take hold of Isadora's hand pulling her to me. Killing her is next to impossible, letting go is next to impossible. What have I gotten myself into?

"You won't, now strip. You can ride."

Her lips turn up at my words as I start removing my clothes and climbing onto the bed. She watches me with unsure eyes, before I reach out and up, pulling at her shirt which she then takes off, followed by her skirt. Within seconds she's climbing into the bed with me. Reaching for her, I put her on top of my hips, she slides over easily without any hassles and sits on my legs with my cock standing tall between us, ready and needing her.

"We shouldn't," she says again but she slides forward.

"You've said that already." I smile, pulling her, her hips push up and when they do, I pull her forward so she's hovering over my cock. "Drop, Isadora. Now!"

Her green eyes lock onto mine. "But I might hurt you."

"You're hurting me right now. Now. Drop," I tell her and it almost stutters out of me. She smiles and reaches between us, positioning my cock at her entrance.

"We should hate each other. No, we should want to kill each other," she says, lowering herself ever so painfully slowly. When she's fully seated, she doesn't move, just looks down at me. "To kill you would have been my greatest revenge." She moves her hips slowly back and forth sliding along my cock.

This is nothing more than painful, blissful, torture.

It's perfection.

It's everything.

"To have you, that will be mine," I say as her hips start to move faster and faster. She doesn't respond to my words, but I know she's heard them. How could she not, I didn't whisper them. And it will, having her will be my ultimate revenge on him, her unscrupulous uncle. But in saying that, it will also be my greatest treasure.

I've not failed her.

It's too late for that.

I fell and no one caught me.

I realized it when I tied her to my father's bed, I didn't want to kill her.

Killing an enemy is easy, that is, unless it's her.

She's impossible to kill.

CHAPTER 27
Isadora

I LAY NEXT to him as he softly snores, watching him. I can't sleep, even though I'm dog tired. I'm too afraid of what tomorrow will bring, and what comes with it.

"Go to sleep." His hand comes over mine, softly holding it, and then he drifts back into a soft snore. Closing my eyes, I feel like I'm almost asleep, that is until a loud bang is heard on the door. When I open my eyes Jasper's already up and walking toward the door. The sun is up. I must have slept and not realized it.

"The uncle is here. The asshole is armed and requesting Isadora."

"Why is he still breathing?" Jasper asks

harshly while pulling on a shirt.

Carter looks to me then to Jasper.

"He has her friend, the one with the kid."

"Oh fuck, no." I jump from the bed not even caring that I'm naked as I reach for the nearest shirt, putting it on without realizing it's Jasper's. Pulling on my skirt, I push past them and run to the mansion where I see Ace standing, holding a gun, pointing it out the door.

"Pink, it's best you don't walk out," he says as I step closer to him.

When I finally get to see, I notice Sharon with a bloody nose, her head hanging low as my uncle holds onto her tightly around the back of her neck with a gun pressed against her rib cage.

I gasp loudly.

Sharon looks up at me, her eyes going wide when she sees me.

"I'm so sorry," I say. She doesn't reply and it's probably best she doesn't.

"You're wearing his shirt. What the fuck is wrong with you?" He spits on the ground. I can clearly see the anger clouding his eyes now.

How did I not see this before?
Was I so blind to it all?

"Let her go." I step forward, but a hand wraps around my waist, pulling me back.

Jasper breathes next to my ear in a whisper, "Don't you dare go any closer to him. Do you

PLAYETTE

understand?" I nod my head at his words.

"Look at you, letting him touch you. Killing everything your mother and father worked for just by being with him."

"You did that, you asshole," I scream. "You wanted their business, it was a bakery. You can't cook. What is wrong with you?" My hands are clenched at my side now.

Poor Sharon cries as Max digs his fingers harder into her neck.

"You ungrateful little bitch. That business was huge. It made a shit ton of money, it was the biggest in this city," he breathes, then looks to Sharon, then back to me, "I paid for you to be the best. You're amazing at what you do, and yet you still fell into this asshole's trap."

"Yeah, I did. Yours. And then I woke up."

My uncle gets mad, pressing the gun to Sharon's temple now, digging in hard while he stares at me.

"I can still make you hate your life. I've already taken what I needed. I have no qualms with taking everything you care about." He clicks the safety, and Sharon's eyes look up, she's pleading with me and there's tears running down her beautiful cheeks.

"She's here," I say out of desperation. It's not my place to say this, but it's the only card I can think of to play to get Sharon away from him right now.

Jasper freezes next to me.

"She's here," I say again.

"Who's here?"

"Leila."

"You're lying." He presses harder and I can see he's pulling back on the trigger.

"I'm not. Jasper never killed her. He locked her up instead. She's here."

My uncle's eyes fall to Jasper for confirmation. I can see the confusion and utter desperation written in his eyes. "You kept her alive?" he asks in disbelief.

"Yes," Jasper says through gritted teeth, his fists clenched to his side. I don't care about his anger right now, knowing this information could save Sharon's life.

"You're fucking lying," he screeches.

I turn around reaching for the key I know is on Jasper's body, and dangle it in the air.

"Do you want to see her?"

"You'll kill me the minute I let this one go."

"Take me then. Let her go, and I'll step into her place."

Jasper reaches for me, but I'm already heading off.

"Let her go, uncle." Uncle Max reaches for me, at the same time he lets Sharon go, and looks at me as he grips my arm so tightly I know it will

PLAYETTE

bruise.

"You should have stayed in your own lane." My uncle then turns the gun to the side of my head and shoots once. Spinning around I watch as Sharon drops to the ground, her eyes open, as the bullet pierces her brain.

Point blank through the skull.

He just killed her.

And it was all my fault.

His hand pulls me along to get me moving. "Walk, Issy. Walk, now." The gun that's just killed Sharon is now digging into my back. "It's all your fault, you know. Her being dead. Your fault," he keeps on rambling as we walk. Jasper steps back, but keeps an eye on my uncle, being careful to not touch him. "Walk faster, Issy, your men are hungry for my blood." He chuckles.

My men?

They aren't my men.

They just don't like it when a crazy son of a bitch kills someone on their property. I walk past the kitchen to the back door which leads downstairs, unlocking it with shaky hands and blurred vision, I almost trip as he pushes me hard down the first set of stairs. How can he be this careless? Was he always like this, and I was just too blind to see it? He never hugged me or kissed my cheek when I was younger telling me I did good, it was always a simple nod of the head and off he went. I tried so hard to please him, and turned myself into what he wanted. And now, now I'm faced with a man I was too blind to see.

Once we're there we come to the second door which I know Jasper's mother is behind. Unlocking it, I step back as she comes into view. She's lying on her single bed with her television turned on as she looks at the wall next to it.

Max pushes me out the way and steps in, going straight to her, wrapping his arms around her body he leans in to kiss her, which she clearly doesn't like, as she tries to push him away. "You're alive," he breathes looking her over.

Jasper comes up behind me and pushes me back so he's now blocking my body, but I can still see.

"Of course I am, you fool. That son of mine was too chicken shit to kill me. Should have, though. Stupid fool that he is."

Max's eyes go wild. "I'm taking you with me." He attempts to pull her, but she yanks her arm free.

"Silly man, I don't love you. Leave. Now." She lays back on the bed, ignoring that he's looking down at her like she's lost her mind. Well, actually, in some ways I guess she has.

"I have ways to support you now. We can live happily."

"Please, I never wanted to be with you, not

PLAYETTE

then, and definitely not now. I just liked testing your boundaries. Tell me, Max, did you do it? Did you kill the little girl, too? I got Jasper's father to kill the family for you." She giggles but it's quite a chilling sound.

Max looks back to me and his face takes on a lost look.

I have no damn sympathy for him. At all.

"What have you done to her?"

"She's sick. She has been for a long time."

Max shakes his head, not liking the sound of that, and starts pacing in the room. Jasper keeps me behind him.

"She was never sick. Leila..." he stops to look at her, "... you aren't sick."

She simply cackles in answer, throwing her head back as she lays on the bed.

"Max, you know one of those house rats you sometimes get? You know the ones, where you train them to do what you want? That's you." Her eyes zoom in on him. "You were like that. I trained you, and made you fall madly in love with me. It's a shame really that the only person not dumb enough to fall for my shit was my son. I guess because he is mine, after all. He has my blood and my character." She laughs looking away from Max, but he starts to grind his teeth.

"What are you talking about?"

"You. You, my dear, were my pet rat. Like

many men before you, and after you. The only man I love is the one who keeps me locked away. Funny how that turned out?" Her eyes fall to Jasper. "I made you who you are. You wouldn't have been as powerful as you are today if it wasn't for me. I made you. You're a made man, son. What a marvelous thing that is." She lays her head on the pillow and looks up at her stars.

I look at Jasper and notice he's as confused as I am.

"You tortured me to make me strong?" He coughs.

Ace and Carter come up behind me. Ace is covered in blood, and I know exactly whose it is without even asking. It's Sharon's.

"Yes, dear, how else could you have made it this far. Gosh, it's past the time to start being thankful."

"You never loved me?" Max asks quietly, so quietly it's almost an unbelieving whisper.

She turns to face him. "What part didn't you understand about you being my pet rat, you idiot?" She huffs.

"I love you. I did all this for you. Fuck this, I'm taking you with me." Uncle Max reaches for her but she pulls her hand away.

"Don't touch me you small, insignificant little rat. Who do you think you are?" She scoffs and sits up then looks over at me, her eyes bearing in

PLAYETTE

on me.

"I've seen you before," she states, then looks at her son. "You love this one?" Jasper doesn't answer, so she cackles. "I wonder how long until you destroy each other? It's what love's great at. Did you know? Love equals destruction."

"I'm not leaving without you," Max states again then he looks back to me and then to Jasper. "What have you done to her?"

Jasper shrugs. "Not a damn thing."

I know Max isn't going to leave this room alive, no matter what. He no longer has any leverage with them and with me because of what he just did to Sharon. Yeah, that's about broken my heart into a thousand irreparable pieces.

"Lies, Leila, get up. You are leaving here." He reaches for her, but she pulls her arm free from him again and spits at him.

"I'm not going anywhere with you. Think again, rat," she barks at him, pulling back even further.

"If you aren't going to come with me..." He raises his gun to Leila's head and she starts cackling.

"Do it, you silly rat. Do it," she screams.

"You really never loved me?" he asks, trying to get it to sit correctly in his mind, while he's still holding the gun to her head.

Jasper's in the doorway still trying to block my

view. Ace steps up and slides a gun past me to Jasper while Max is not looking.

"No, I used you. As I did everyone in my life. I was put on this earth to make *him.*" She looks to Jasper with a soft smile. "You were just some fun I had along the way."

Max shoots, the same way he shot Sharon.

Jasper's mother falls to the bed with a sickening thud.

Max looks our way as Jasper shoots.

Max falls to the floor with a thud so loud, I think it will echo through my ears for years to come.

Jasper steps into the room and heads straight to his mother. His hand touches her face and he closes her eyes with his fingers. "I'm sorry," he whispers then leans down to kiss her cheek. My heart breaks for him as he stands up and kicks Max's dead body on the floor.

Jasper looks at me then walks straight past me not saying a word as he leaves.

I desperately want him to turn back around and tell me everything will be all right even though I know it won't. But he doesn't, he doesn't even glance back at me. That hurts more then I care to admit right now.

"Issy." I turn to Carter who hands me a set of keys. "It's time you left." I look at him, and then to the keys, unsure of what's going on. Taking the

PLAYETTE

keys, he nods to me before he walks into the room where both the bodies lay. Taking a deep breath, I try to tell myself I can do this. That today hasn't been as crazy as it now seems. I've managed to get Sharon killed and now my uncle as well.

No. This did not happen.

Did it?

Walking up the stairs and into the kitchen area, I look out the back to Jasper's house. I know he is in there, I can see his silhouette, but it's probably best I leave.

A car sits out front, it's a small red one, and when I click the keys I know it's the one I'm meant to leave in. I turn back to see if Jasper's come out to say goodbye.

He hasn't.

And Sharon's body, which laid right here on this ground, is no longer there either.

CHAPTER 28
Jasper

Pacing back and forth my fists clench and unclench.

I knew a day like this was coming. My mother couldn't stay in that room for the rest of her life. But I didn't think I'd be there to witness her demise.

She's dead, and I watched it happen.

Looking down, blood covers my hands. *Her* blood.

I loved my mother.

I also hated her.

She didn't understand the meaning of love, and her way of loving me was cruel and not what any child should have to endure. I've seen a lot in this world, and I'm a part of the bad and will forever be. That won't change.

Children for me, they're off-limits.

Always.

I'll never put a child through this.

"Sharon has a child," Ace says opening the door, he's also covered in blood. Not *her* blood. No. It's Sharon's blood.

"Go. Make sure she has what she needs. Set her up for life." He nods, walking out, pulling his phone to his ear as he leaves.

That insignificant man ruined my life, not just by killing *her*, but for Isadora as well. If I could un-kill and torture him some more I fucking would. I would do it in a heartbeat.

Max loved a woman who didn't love him back. He was too blind to see it, too stupid to know better. And in the process, he killed those that actually loved him. Who would have done anything for him.

Washing my hands, I watch as the blood washes down the sink and takes my emotion with it. Mother's better off, she was sick. I should have done it all those years ago, but she wasn't as easy to kill as my father was. I know she was vindictive, but I loved her.

When I go back to the mansion, the clean-up crew has already arrived and are sweeping up

PLAYETTE

the mess. Body bags are being taken out, and I stop when I know it's *her*. My hand touches her body over the top of the black bag.

"Cremate her, and bring *her* back to me." The cleaner nods and continues to go about his business.

"I sent Isadora away. You need space from her," Carter says. He's my second in command for a reason. He sees clearly when I don't.

"Do you think that's smart?"

"You tell me? You wanted to kill her, but couldn't. You took a bullet for her then you watched as her uncle killed your mother. So, you tell me, was it the best option?" He shakes his head and starts walking out of the room.

"She's more to me than just a pussy, Carter. Watch yourself."

His back straightens. "We know this. She knows this. Let it breathe, and when you both have had time to grieve then go back to each other and see what's there. Right now, it isn't smart."

"And you know about love, do you?" I ask him raising an eyebrow.

He laughs. "I love you, boss. I'd give my life for you. No one else matters above you. But that is the life I choose. You didn't. So you can love more than us. Fuck, you can have her if you want even if she doesn't want you. It's you. It's all about you. Who are we to stop you. But all I ask is that you let yourself breathe for a moment. You need that. Just breathe. Take some well-earned time off. You've been consumed by her, and I personally don't understand it." He walks away leaving me standing where I am, watching the space he vacated.

When I was a teenager, before I killed my father. What I wanted most in this life was a wife. One who I could count on. One who wouldn't ruin me or use me. I figured out later that it was next to impossible to find something like that in this life. Especially considering who I am, and the power I hold. But that dream, it still niggles at the back of my throat when I'm near Isadora. Could she be it?

No, she can't be. She started a war and never finished it.

Though, this wasn't all her, and despite everything that's happened I still very much want her.

She's exactly what I fantasized about. She was the woman stuck in my dreams, and when I found her I knew I had to have her, it was simply hard to work out how. With so much bad, so much ugly, how could it ever really work?

Dreams are meant to be altered, and mine was, tremendously.

Max's body comes up last. "Burn that one or feed it to the wolves, I don't fucking care," I say

PLAYETTE

pointing to her Uncle. If I could kill him, again and again, I would. The cleaner nods then walks out with some of my other men.

This life I live is one where I run, and profit, from the businesses around me. I own half of them, and if I don't, you can bet I soon will.

My father took this town with force, scaring the locals, but I run it with good business sense. Bought them out, and made sure they knew not to cross me. Some I loaned money to, knowing full well they couldn't pay me back, but their business was always my collateral.

The strip club where I found Isadora.

Benny. He's not one of the brightest lights in the sky. I did the same thing with him, but at least he still runs it. Benny most definitely isn't my biggest fan, but he doesn't need to be.

"Do you intend to do anything?" Ace asks, pulling his shirt over his head.

"Yes, I plan to burn Max's place to the ground."

Ace nods.

And that's what we do.

Go straight to that shithole where Max lived. We walk in, spilling accelerant all over the floor, and then removing the cars. I can sell them. As I said, I'm a businessman, I'm not stupid. I have plenty of cars both old and new alike, and they're like a passion for me.

Walking up the stairs to the rooms, I come to an office first. Clearly this is where that bastard looked after the business. Behind that is three rooms, the first is a bathroom, the second is Isadora's.

A photo of Isadora and her family hang on the wall. I remember them all clearly. It's hard to forget something like that. Not that I hadn't been around killing before, but in the manner where my father didn't care, I hadn't noticed that in him before that fateful day. He laughed when he shot Isadora's mother, then smiled when he shot her father.

Isadora looks like her mother, she has the same green eyes as well as her hair. But her face is more like her father's. I take the picture from its frame and step out of the room. There's nothing else here other than clothes and a mattress on the floor.

Walking into the next room, this one has a mattress on the floor as well, but what is different is it has more. Clothes and more pictures, but these pictures consist of my mother, Max and Isadora. This shit makes me angry. There's not one picture of the person he's supposedly revenging. He did it all for the wrong reasons.

I don't like Isadora's actions, but I'm no one to judge. I'm worse than she will ever be. Stepping out, I light a match flicking it on the floor before I walk out.

PLAYETTE

From the front, I watch as it goes up in flames and continue to watch while the whole fucking place burns to the fucking ground.

And with it the memory of my father.

"You listen, son, and you fucking listen good." My father smacked the back of my head hard. I'm in his room after he just killed another man for no fucking good reason.

Carter stepped out of the room as my father's voice raised, and knew full well what kind of man he was about to be.

"When I order you to kill the little guy, you fucking kill him. Do you understand me?" He pointed a finger in my face, flashing around his gold skull ring.

"No," I argued back.

That wasn't going to happen. He should be locked up and put away for being the asshole he was. But he owned every crooked detective and every dishonest lawyer in this town. No one would dare touch him.

"You ungrateful little fucking shit, you're meant to be a man now. Did you lose your cock when you fucked that last whore?" he spat, slapping me across my face.

I loved him so much once. He'd changed, though. I guess, in my story, they all do. It was the sad reality of life. No one stayed the same.

"You're getting bad in your old age, old man," I seethed back at him.

That was the last straw.

Kill the little guy, because he walked in on my father after he'd killed his father and stepped over his body and screamed.

Kids. I don't do kids.

It's not their fault they were born into this awful fucking world.

"You think 'cause you're eighteen now you're a man?" My father's head fell back as he laughed. "No. You aren't," he said standing tall. He removed his gun, placing it on his bedside table. Fuck, this place was like a museum. It's all fucking gold, and I hated it. "What could make you a man is something you will never accomplish. You're your mother's boy. What a fucking shame."

He hated her, but when she wanted something, he was the first to do it for her. Their relationship was fucked and something I never wanted for my future.

"I'll be more of a man than you'll ever be."

He laughed, shaking his head. "Son, that you will never be. And I hope one day you fall in love with a woman who fucks it all up for you. Just as mine's done for me." He turned, walking to his dresser, then back to his bed. Removing his clothes, he sat on the edge to pull off his shoes, and that's when I knew what I had to do.

It had to be done.

The bastard had to be killed.

No matter what.

No matter the consequences.

Raising the gun in my hand to his head, he looked

PLAYETTE

up at me, and with laughing eyes he went back to what he was doing.

"I raised you right, but you do have your mother in you, after all. So crazy runs in your blood, but you won't kill me, son. That would mean you will have to take over the business, and that's something you don't want."

He was right. I didn't want that responsibility this young. But I had more respect from his men then he did, and the ones who were loyal to him I planned to kill anyway. They were just as fucked in the head as he was.

"You can't keep doing this," I said while shaking my head slowly.

"Wrong! I can and I will."

I didn't say anything back to that, and I didn't drop the gun either.

"You think the power won't go to your head? It does. People like us can't help ourselves. It's in our damn blood, son."

"No. We can help ourselves, and killing people just because you feel like it needs to stop. You're ruining everything," I said.

He went to push the gun away, but I kept it in place. Standing, he pushed the end of the gun into his chest. "It's addictive… the killing. Soon they'll all blend together, and you will want to keep doing it. When you become that man, think of me and smile, son. Now do it before I take the gun off you, and put a bullet to your brain. Just remember as you pull that *trigger, I love you."*

I didn't bother asking him if he was speaking the truth. He'd lost all sense of who he was, and I sometimes wondered why I was still alive in this place.

"I love you."

He nodded his head as I pulled back on the trigger. Falling backward, he landed on his bed, his hand going to his chest where the bullet entered. His door opened and his second in command stepped inside with wide eyes. He raised his gun at me, but before he could do anything he fell to the floor. Carter stood behind him holding a knife which he'd just lodged in his throat.

"Boss," Carter said with a nod. "Should I call the clean-up crew?"

I nodded and stayed in the room until they arrived.

Carter was the only one to come in, as I sat on the bed next to my father, knowing full well that everything was about to change.

"No one is to come in here. Ever. After this room is cleaned it's never to be touched again. The rest of the house is yours," I told Carter.

He nodded as I walked out.

And just like that I had killed my father, and I had become the boss.

All my worst nightmares had just come to life.

CHAPTER 29
Isadora

Two months later.

BELLA SMILES AS I walk in, she could light up a room with that smile.

"You're back. Felt like you've been gone for ages," she says, collapsing onto her bed.

"Only a week," I tell her touching her hair.

Sharon had a mother which she hardly spoke to who took full custody of Bella. I try to visit her at least once a week, bringing her something special every time.

As soon as I left that day, I went straight to

Sharon's house. Looked around inside until I found her mother's phone number in a drawer and called her to let her know she'd have to collect Bella today from daycare.

Sharon's death was deemed an accident, even though I know the truth. The guilt is something I will never be rid of. Ever.

Jasper's helped with that. I haven't seen him once in the last two months, but he messages me with words of comfort and sends me things, but he's not once left my mind.

I like getting to know him in a situation where he doesn't control the outcome, and his hands don't make me forget my situation.

The trouble is he's good at that.

Making me forget.

Heather, well, I haven't seen her again. And I hope I never do. I never want to take a life again, but hers, I would seriously contemplate killing her.

And the men I murdered, the guilt that resides inside of me because of that, will never die, but I have learned to live with it. It is out of my control, and I was being controlled by someone whose motives weren't in my best interest. That was hard for me to come to terms with.

"How's school?" I ask

Bella shrugs her shoulders as a little puppy comes running into the room.

PLAYETTE

"Who's this?" I ask, leaning over and picking him up. He licks my face as Bella laughs.

"Jasper got him for me."

I place the dog down as I look at her. "Jasper?" I ask, confused.

She nods her head. "He said the puppy will make me happy, and he was right. The puppy makes me very happy, but not so much Grandma, when he pees and poos everywhere." She offers me a small giggle before she goes off chasing him around the room.

Leaving, I check my phone and see a message from him.

It's time, don't you think?

My heart rate speeds up at the thought of seeing him again, and what I might feel. My life has changed so much, I no longer have any need for revenge. I don't think I could do that ever again anyway. It drained me as a person. It took away my identity and majorly interfered with my personality. I've been trying to find work, and figure out what I want to do with my life.

My parents wanted me to be a lawyer, but I dedicated my life to avenging them thanks to my uncle.

So, who am I, if I'm not that person?

Who is Isadora? The woman. My identity. My whole self.

I'm still trying to figure out those questions.

I smile climbing into *my* car. I sent their car back to them and bought my own with the money I had saved. I have a lot put away from the fire that happened at Max's garage. So much so, I'm not sure what to do with it.

The fire was investigated, and thankfully I was nowhere near it at the time, so it was cleared for the insurance money.

Maybe.

I start the car and when I do my phone beeps again.

I'm behind you Isadora. Start driving to the local *café*.

I turn around, and sure enough, Jasper's in the passenger seat of a black sedan following behind me. Ace smiles and offers me a wave before I spin around. Pulling away from the house, I drive to the closest *café* and pull up.

Getting out, my maxi dress sways at my feet as I wait for him to walk over. He doesn't disappoint when he greets me with his hands in his pockets, glasses covering his eyes and with those lips with that scar. When he reaches me, I remember to breathe, taking a deep breath, one at a time. I look from his shoes, shiny black ones, up to his dark denim jeans until I reach his chest, broad and everything I've missed.

"Isadora," he says and I swear it knocks the air

PLAYETTE

out of my lungs. "It's been a minute." I nod as he looks behind me then back to me. "Coffee?" He nods to the *café in front of us*.

"Sure."

Jasper steps back from my personal space and waves for me to walk in first.

A waitress comes over and he places both our orders as we sit.

"I've missed you. Who would've thought it, right?"

"You missed me?" I ask, surprised.

He nods, confirming it. "Did you miss me, Isadora?"

I nod. "Very much so."

"Good, I'm glad that's settled. So, when can I expect you to move in with me?"

I balk at his words and shake my head, confused. "What? Move in with you?" I ask him, shocked.

"Yes. You hate that place, and it still looks like you don't live there. Don't you want to make something your own? My place can be that."

I didn't live in that shithole for living there, though. My place was with my uncle, and now, well, I don't even like to think of him anymore or even care about what happened to everything we once had there. It all went up in smoke, and he deserved that even in his death.

"We haven't even seen each other in ages.

How do you know you still even want me? And, for your information, moving in with you is not making *your* place my own."

"I know what I want. I've always wanted you. It was never a question, Isadora, it was a matter of questioning if I could fit you into my life. You did destroy so much of it."

I look down as a waiter comes over, placing coffee in front of us.

"I'm sorry. So very sorry about that."

"I get it. I get why you did what you did. I would have done the same. Don't apologize, Isadora. Just move on and do better."

"Don't you think we should go slow, though?"

He laughs. "No. I've never done anything slow, and I don't plan to do you slow either."

I choke on my drink because I know exactly what that means.

"Exactly," he says as I wipe my mouth.

"I'm not moving in. Not yet. I need… time."

"I've given you months."

"We both needed that," I reply.

"Yes, but now I'm over it, and I need you back. I'm not a patient man, Isadora, not sure how much longer I can wait." He doesn't touch his coffee, instead he watches me with intent while waiting for me to speak. *Do I hold the power here?* Jasper isn't one who gives power away, he always holds on to it tightly. So this is new. Very

PLAYETTE

new.

"I'm sorry about your mother," I say, remembering what my uncle did.

"It's fine. She had to die anyway. It was probably easier than me doing it." He shrugs.

"Still, you loved her."

"I love you."

My eyes go wide at his words.

No, he can't mean that.

Can he?

"You can't possibly. You don't know me," I say, shaking my head.

He leans in and touches my knee, holds me with his hand. "I know what I need to know, the rest we can work out along the way."

"What if you find out I hate cats, and you love cats. Or worse, I'm allergic to seafood and you love it?" I ask.

"If you hate cats, I will deal. If you're allergic to seafood, I will never eat it around you, or come home and mouth fuck you."

I giggle at his words. "I'm still not moving in with you," I tell him. "Slower. We need slower."

He nods and agrees. "Tonight then. You can come tonight?"

I nod and he smiles. We both stand.

When we walk outside to my car, Ace is standing there having a cigarette. When he sees me, he smiles and nods his head in hello. "Isadora."

I stop outside of my car and turn back to face Jasper. "Don't be late. I look forward to seeing you."

His eyes roam over me. "Dressed in less."

I blush, I know I do. So, I quickly hop into the car, shutting the door, and driving off.

It's as I remember it, the mansion hasn't changed, but it's not as busy. Or maybe that's just tonight. Walking up to the front door I knock twice before it's opened. Jasper stands there dressed in a suit, looking hot.

His eyes roam me up and down in my red dress. I went and purchased it especially for tonight. I'm nervous, so fucking nervous. It's been ages since I've seen him, and even longer since we've been on a date.

Is that what this is? Fuck! I don't even know, I've never dated.

It was always sex for me. Sex was what I liked, so why play around with the small talk and dinner or movies.

"Well, fuck." He offers me his hand, I place mine in his. He pulls me inside the house, his hand staying in mine as we walk. "You look…" He looks to me, shaking his head before turning back around. "You look real good, Isadora."

PLAYETTE

I smile as we walk through the mansion and out the back to where his house is located.

"You look good, too," I say. The suit he's wearing looks incredible on him, showing all the right curves of his body. Black does everything for him, with a touch of white only on his tie.

"It's for you, to impress you into never leaving."

I chuckle at his words, and he spins around to look at me. "I like the sound of that." His fingers drop from mine as he steps over to his fridge, and that's when I look around. The place appears the same apart from the table which is set up for just the two of us. A candle sits in the middle with two white plates and rose petals scattered all over the floor.

"You did all of this?" I smile, walking over and sitting at the table. He steps over with a bottle of wine in his hand, and a smile I've missed so badly.

"Yes, for you."

"You didn't have to."

"Yes, I know. But you and me, well, we have history that's not good. So this… this is our way of starting afresh."

"Do you think we can ever forgive and forget?" I ask him.

"I've already forgiven you, Isadora. I did that the minute I tied you to my father's bed. It's the forgetting we both will have trouble with, and if we didn't, we should probably be tied to that bed again." He steps closer and pours me a glass of wine then looks down at me. "You are quite perfect for me." The bottle of wine is put on the table, his hand comes under my chin lifting it, so he now has my full attention. "I've worked out that I can kiss these lips…" and he does just that, with a brush of his own, "… for the rest of my life, and still be a happy man." He pulls away and takes a seat across from me.

"The question remains, can you be happy with me? Knowing full well what I do and who I am?"

"If you would've asked me that months ago, my answer would have been a firm no. Everything you are is what I'm against. But I realize now that those thoughts were controlled and not my own. So, yes, Jasper… I could kiss those broken lips of yours for a very long time." He pulls the lid off a large tray and beneath it is pasta and bread. I smile as we start to eat.

Our conversation comes easy and natural, and not once does he ask me what I've been up to. I have a feeling he already knows that anyway.

"I have something for you." Jasper stands, walking away to his room, then he comes back and hands me something. Taking it from him, I turn it over and see my parents. It was the only photo of them I kept, and I kept it in the room above the garage at my uncle's. So I assumed it

PLAYETTE

was gone.

"You burned it down."

He merely nods.

"Thank you for this. Really. I know you didn't have to, so I thank you." I get up and wrap my arms around his neck holding him tight. He does the same, holding me to him and I even hear him breathe me in.

"I would pretty much do anything for you, Isadora. So, burning that place down was for you, not for me." I squeeze a little tighter and he pushes back without moving our hands away from each other. He looks at me, and I feel like he can actually see me. The real me. The person. Who I am. The one who's still trying to figure myself out, without the world I've become accustomed to.

"I haven't had someone who wants me, for me, in a very long time. The only people who were my friends, have died," I say telling him the truth and also letting him know who I am. I'm not used to anything he's after. I've never had it, so this is all very new to me. If I wanted sex before I would have it simply for the fun and the release, not because I saw anything going further with the person I was sleeping with. With Jasper, I want sex with him for different reasons, because as a man he makes me want more.

Moving my hands from his shoulders to his

face I cup it and lean in to kiss his lips. I feel the jagged edge of his scar on my lip and I love it. I know these lips, I will forever be branded by these lips, for all eternity, of that I am sure.

Lips move fast, hands roam to my back, then slide down to my ass. The desire I feel for him is next-level crazy. I like the way he evokes that in me. The passion, I've only ever felt it with him. And I like that feeling.

Jasper's hands lift my ass and I wrap my legs around his waist as he carries me. He places my ass on the table, pushing everything off and onto the floor, and smiles down at me as we separate. He doesn't waste any time before his shirt, which was perfectly buttoned, but is now button-less, is pulled off and he's back in front of me.

This is the man who I've come to love.

Yes.

Love.

The time we spent apart confirmed it, told me each and every day, because he was on my mind more than any other person before him.

I quite enjoy it, being consumed by one man.

He pulls my perfect red dress up my thighs and to my waist. When he sees I have nothing on underneath, he bites his lip, looking up at me with a smirk.

"Naughty…"

I nod at his words.

PLAYETTE

"I'm going to fuck you fast and hard, then after, I will take my time. But for now, I just need you."

I reach for him, and he comes forward, his cock between my legs is begging at my entrance, as I start kissing his lips. He pushes inside of me and I feel him stretch me. The minute he's fully inside me, my lips forget to move and a large moan leaves my mouth.

"That's my girl." He bites my bottom lip and comes up, so he's looking down over me and he starts moving fast and hard, pushing in and out, his fingers digging into my hips to keep me on the table while he takes what I have to give.

It's punishment, in its best form.

It's love, in its most sensual form.

It's everything I've missed and never knew I wanted.

Jasper leans down and kisses the side of my neck and whispers in my ear, "I love you."

If I wasn't already close to losing my breath from my orgasm building, it's completely gone now.

"Tell me you missed me, Isadora." His hand slides to my neck, and he applies slight pressure, while his pace never slows. "Tell me. Tell me, now."

"I missed you."

"How much?" he asks, slowing his rhythm,

waiting for me to give him the answers he wants. Needs.

"So much."

"Did it hurt to breathe without me?" he asks, and then he stops moving.

Damn it, I'm so close, so close that I try to move, but he has me pinned and it's almost impossible to shift at all.

"I love you, too. Is that what you want to hear?" I ask, while staring up to the ceiling.

Those words have never left my mouth, for a man, and not for a very long time other than that. It almost hurts, or tears something open inside of me that I didn't realize I had closed tightly shut.

"Yes, it's what I want to hear, you need to say it. Trust me, if anyone knows, it's me."

He starts moving again, but this time he isn't fast as he leans down and kisses my lips with each slow movement pulling my orgasm from me. "I've missed you terribly, Isadora." Jasper stands upright, my hands find the edge again, and grip it hard as his pace picks back up. I take what he's giving and soon my eyes are squeezing shut and my hands are going white from gripping the table so hard. "Don't ever leave me again."

"I won't," I reply, and I mean it. I don't want to leave him ever again. He's where I feel I want to be.

PLAYETTE

He is it.

Home for me.

Two fucked-up people can make it work. *Can't they?*

There has to be hope for the broken, too.

CHAPTER 30
Isadora

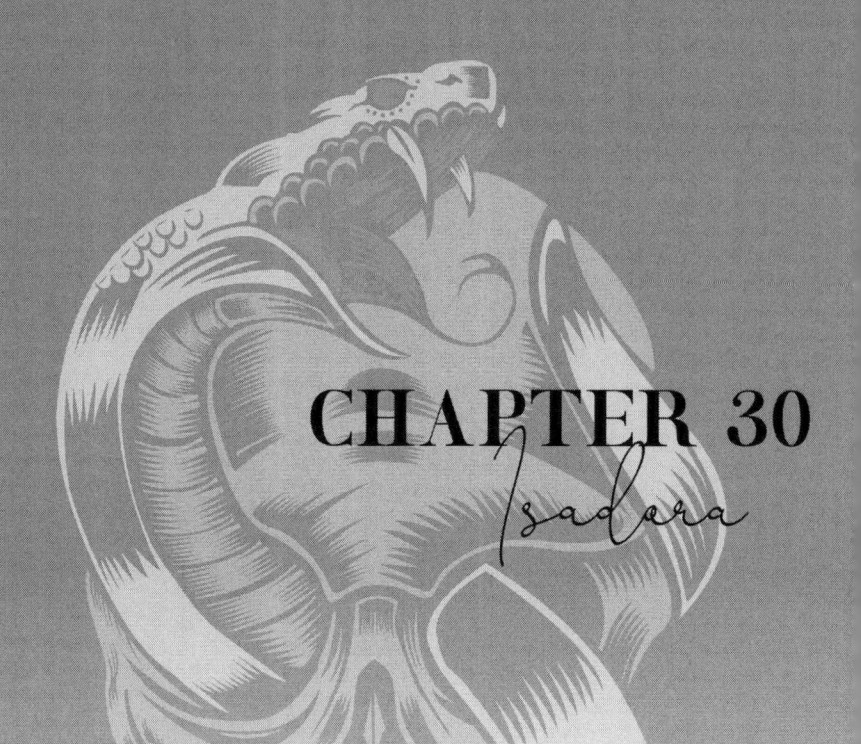

I LEFT, I had to. I didn't want to move in with Jasper straight away, even if he would have liked it that way.

It's too soon for me. I want to do the second time around right.

Well, as right as we possibly can.

It's been three weeks now, and each and every time he tries to get me to stay. Most of my clothes are there, so I do practically live there, but I'm trying to let him breathe to make sure I don't suffocate him either. It needs to be right, no wrong moves by either of us.

I hear a knock on the door of my small room,

and I know who it is before I even open it. Same time almost every day he's here to collect me. I argued a few times that we needed our space, to make sure that we're doing this right. He laughed and slept in my bed. That was his idea of considering me having some space.

Opening the door, he's there, smiling. My heart skips a beat, pounding so loud, I'm surprised he doesn't hear it.

"I've missed you." His hands wrap around my waist, pulling me to him.

"You saw me this morning," I say, wrapping my arms around his shoulders and leaning in to kiss him.

"You make me come here, when you could easily live with me. Isadora, when I get home it's you I want to see, so I come straight here."

"Here isn't so bad, is it?" I kiss his lips again.

"It is. It's fucking awful. Now pack your shit and move in with me already, woman."

"Ask me nicely," I say, smiling.

He pinches my ass. "Fuck it! I'll move you in myself."

"So demanding." I roll my eyes.

"You bet. Now hurry up. Have you finished work for the day?" I nod, pulling away before going to grab my bag. I look around at the few things I have left. I've never made this place a home, it's never felt like one. Jasper's home, on

PLAYETTE

the other hand, has me written all over it.

"Yep, and maybe tomorrow I'll grab the rest of my things, and we can make this thing official," I say.

He smiles.

Big.

"You mean it?"

I nod as he pulls me in and dips me, so I squeal.

I know work for him has been good. I'm not into any of the illegal side of his businesses. Instead, I look after the staff at the night club and help Benny out, but Jasper asks that I don't strip or dance for another soul apart from him. I agree, he's the only person I like to dance for anyway.

"Yes, I prefer it at yours."

"Ours," he corrects me.

"It's too soon to marry you, right? That's probably throwing you off, correct? Move in one day, marry you the next?"

My eyes go wide.

Fuck!

Marriage.

Shit!

That's not something I've ever thought about. Ever.

Truth be told, I expected to die after I accomplished what I had planned. Now, I'm simply enjoying life and that just so happens to be with Jasper.

"Okay, okay, I take it back. No marriage. Yet." He leans down, grabbing my bag and walking out. "But I'm going to tell you, I dreamt of you, before I saw you. So, I know, soon you will marry me."

Shock glues me to the floor, my feet unable to move as he walks out. *Did he just say what I think he did?* Marriage? I never saw that in my future. Now, I guess I should.

Ace is standing out the front, smirking when he sees me. I know he's trying to contain his laughter. I've become good friends with him, and really enjoy his company. He's very compassionate, so much more than I originally thought.

"Don't you laugh." I hit his chest walking past him, but he drops over in fits of laughter.

"Did she freak out? Tell me what her face looked like?" he asks Jasper.

I've come to learn and understand their dynamic. They don't just see Jasper as their boss, they respect and love him as well. He's so much more to them, so much more than just a boss. He's their form of a god.

I get it, he is godlike after all. But if you look closely, you can see the cracks that were marked on him specifically to make him the man he is today.

PLAYETTE

"Oh yeah, she's still white," Jasper says jokingly while opening the door.

Ace climbs into the driver seat.

"Fuck you both." I flip them off.

Climbing in, Jasper leans down and kisses my lips. "It's okay, Isadora, there's still tomorrow." He shuts the door and walks around to slide in, while Ace continues to laugh.

Jasper did the same thing with trying to get me to move in with him, he asked me every single day. I guess it worked. Because here I am agreeing to move in with him.

"Don't you dare ask tomorrow. It's slow, remember?"

He laughs, and I know he will.

Jasper will keep on asking until I agree.

And he will win.

Why wouldn't he? He owns my heart.

OTHER BOOKS BY
T.L. Smith

Sasha's Dilemma (Dilemma #1) FREE
Adam's Heaven (Dilemma #1.5)
Sasha's Demons (Dilemma #2)
Kandiland
Pure Punishment (Standalone)
Antagonize Me (Standalone)

Degrade (Flawed #1)
Twisted (Flawed #2)

Black (Black #1)
Red (Black #2)
White (Black #3)
Green (Black #4)

Distrust (Smirnov Bratva #1) FREE
Disbelief (Smirnov Bratva #2)
Defiance (Smirnov Bratva #3)
Dismissed (Smirnov Bratva #4)

OTHER BOOKS BY
T.L. Smith

Lovesick (Standalone)
Lotus (Standalone)

Savage Collision (A Savage Love Duet book 1)
Savage Reckoning (A Savage Love Duet book 2)
Buried in Lies
Distorted Love (Dark Intentions Duet 1)
Sinister Love (Dark Intentions Duet 2)
Cavalier (Crimson Elite #1)
Anguished (Crimson Elite #2)
Conceited (Crimson Elite #3)
Insolent (Crimson Elite #4)

Connect with T.L Smith at
www.tlsmithauthor.com

Printed in Great Britain
by Amazon